Hiding Out In The Mountains

Greene Mountain Boys

Olivia T. Turner

www.OliviaTTurner.com

Edited by Karen Collins Editing
Cover Design by Olivia T. Turner

To my mystical muse who helps me come up with all these stories.
He's hot as fuck and his dick is enormous.

Chapter One

Ruby

Does it ever fucking end?

That's a question I've been asking myself a lot lately. I ask it again when I walk into my sketchy apartment building and see the handwritten *Out of Order* sign taped to the elevator.

It's one in the morning and I've been working since five AM. I don't have the energy to walk up seven flights of stairs right now. I don't even have the energy to wash my face.

I take a deep breath and head to the stairwell. This building is in one of the worst areas of Seattle and it's full of people you don't want to run into in a stairwell at one o'clock in the morning. I don't have much of a choice though, so I suck it up and head inside.

So far, so good. There's tons of graffiti on the wall, broken beer bottles everywhere, and cigarette butts shamelessly tossed about, but no people. I quickly work my way up the stairs.

My feet are killing. Every day starts at five AM at the diner where I seat people and answer the phones. After my eight-hour shift, I race home to work on my custom sticker shop that I've been struggling to get off the ground. It took me three years to scrounge together six thousand dollars for the equipment to make custom stickers that people order from my online shop. I put together the orders—if I have any—and then race to the post office to deliver them before it closes. From there, I head to the Chinese restaurant where I work as a delivery girl.

The days are long but the years are... also long. I've been working all kinds of crappy jobs since I was sixteen years old. I'm twenty-two now and I'm hoping this sticker business is my way out.

I'm determined to make it work. I busted my ass for years to buy a high-end printer and an expensive cutting machine to give my customers the very best stickers I can make. For the first time in a long time, I can see the light at the end of the tunnel.

My business might work out.

Does it ever fucking end?

Maybe... Maybe soon.

I breathe in a little sigh of relief when I arrive on the seventh floor. I didn't run into any of the future convicts who live in my building along the way, so I'm counting that as a win.

This is a rough neighborhood and I'm always looking over my shoulders, fearing for my safety. It doesn't help that I'm alone in life. No family, no friends besides the acquaintances I have at work, and definitely no boyfriend. It's my job to keep myself safe. No one else's. It would be nice to have someone looking out for me for a change, but that's not the hand I was dealt.

I crack the door to the main hallway and listen for voices with my key sticking out of my fist like that's going to do a damn thing to anyone out there. A baby is crying from one of the apartments and there's some loud bass vibrating through the walls, but no one seems to be in the hallway.

God, I hate it here.

One day, when my sticker business takes off, I'm going to move to a place where I don't have to fear for my life every time I take the garbage out.

But that day is not today, so I push the door open and hurry down the hallway to my apartment. I glance over my shoulder as I go. There's a new graffiti symbol tagged on the wall and someone ripped up a portion of the carpet. Lovely.

My heart slows as I arrive at my door. But just as I'm about to shove my key into the lock, a door at the end of the hall bursts open.

I jump up and gasp as a frantic man with a shaved head and wide bulging eyes explodes out of it. He runs down the hall like he's just seen a monster. He's tall and lanky, wearing baggy jeans and a dirty undershirt. His lean muscles are clenched tight over his pale sweaty skin.

He doesn't even notice that I'm standing here as he sprints by me.

"No!" he screams as he looks back in horror at the open door.

The monster emerges.

Crenshaw.

I don't know what he does for a living, but I'm sure it involves a lot of meth, guns, and dead bodies. He's wearing a black suit—no tie—and a white shirt in a style that can only be described as drug dealer chic. He lowers his head, peering forward over his dark sunglasses. His greasy hair is slicked back and he hasn't shaven in days.

Gun! Holy shit, he has a gun!

I flatten myself against the door as he stalks forward and raises the pistol in his hand. Those dark sinister eyes are glaring at the fleeing man.

A loud *POP* rockets through my brain and makes my heart nearly leap out of my chest. The fleeing man falls forward as a ringing hits my ears. He slams into the ground face-first, making no effort to break his fall.

That's when I see a small coin-sized hole in the back of his head spurting out blood.

I gasp as I turn back to the man who pulled the trigger.

Two more guys rush out and run past Crenshaw. One has a large Ziplock bag in his hand.

I feel like I've stepped out of my body as I watch them run up to the dead man and wrap the plastic bag around his head. It fills with blood immediately.

"Grab his legs," one of them barks at the other.

They drag him back down the hallway and disappear into the apartment. It's over as quickly as it started. There's barely a drop of blood on the ground.

A girl joins Crenshaw in the hallway. She's about my age with tight shredded-up jeans and a black shirt. She reeks of trauma and bad decisions.

I suck in a sharp breath when I realize they're both looking at me.

Crenshaw is terrifying. I was warned about staying away from him from a nice older lady in the apartment building when I moved in and now I can see why.

Those cold heartless eyes are locked on me. He's a psychopath. A killer. My body vibrates with alarm bells as our eyes meet.

An overwhelming sense of dread hits me like I'm a baby deer who's suddenly been spotted by a large hungry wolf.

But some things in the world are worse than wolves, and Crenshaw is one of them. He's a demon in human flesh.

He takes off his sunglasses and holds them over his shoulder. His girlfriend takes them without a word and he starts stalking toward me.

Oh shit!

My heart races and my mouth goes bone dry as I whip around and fumble with my key. He starts running toward me as I finally shove it into the door, yank it to the side, and turn the handle. I dart inside, slam the door closed, and lock it just as he arrives.

The banging starts immediately.

"Open up!" he hollers in a deep voice that makes the tiny hairs on my arms rise. "Open the fucking door!"

"No, thank you!" I shout back.

The banging gets louder. Harder.

He's kicking the door down!

I clutch my purse and run through my tiny apartment to the back door. I unlock it, whip it open, and race onto my balcony. My building has those old-fashioned metal fire escapes and I immediately start running down them. I was worried that these would be horrible for security when I moved in, but I'm relieved that I have them now.

I pass some thugs hanging out on their balconies on the way down, but I just keep running past them, even as they holler after me.

My heart is racing and my lungs are on fire when I finally get to the second floor. The ladder is pulled up and I have to jump down a few feet, but I land on the concrete without hurting myself.

I'm dizzy with fear and my heart is thrashing in my ears when I look up at the seventh floor.

Crenshaw bursts onto my balcony and looks right at me.

Our eyes meet over the vast distance. His narrow. Mine widen.

"Stay *right* there!" he shouts in a gravelly voice.

He turns around and sprints back into my apartment.

Yeah, *fuuuuccck* that!

I squeeze my keys in my hand and run as fast as I can to my car. It's on the other side of the building, but it's still much closer than the distance Crenshaw has to go.

"Please, please, please, please," I whisper over and over as I run to it. Sometimes it can take a while to get it started. I'm really hoping this is not one of those times.

I unlock the door, hop in, and turn the key in the ignition as I stare at the front door, expecting the devil to burst out at any moment. The engine starts on the first try and I peel out of the parking lot as fast as I can.

I spot Crenshaw exploding out of the building as I pull onto the street, but I hit the gas and disappear into the guts of the city before he can get to his car and follow me.

When I'm far enough across town that I'm sure he's not on my tail, I pull over and struggle to get my breathing and heart rate under control. It takes a while, but I finally settle down.

The hopeless reality of my situation hits me hard and I drop my head onto the steering wheel, wanting to cry.

"What am I supposed to do now?"

He's probably ransacking my apartment. He's probably sitting on my couch, waiting for me to return. I'm so fucked.

Sooooo fucked.

I start really missing my dad. Warm tears flow out.

They stream down my steering wheel and onto my lap as I break down in sobs.

He was the toughest guy I know. He was a decorated Navy SEAL before he got killed in action when I was only sixteen.

If he was still alive, I'd run to him and he would take care of me. He would have taken care of everything.

But he's gone now and I have no one left to look out for me.

Not true...

It's a little voice in the back of my head. An optimistic tone peeking out of the darkness.

You can always run to Jack.

I take a breath and raise my head at the memory of my dad's best friend. I can still remember exactly how he looked in his uniform at my dad's funeral.

"You can always count on me, Ruby," he whispered as he took my hand and gazed into my eyes. "I'll always be here for you."

He's all the way in Montana. The Greene Mountains if I recall correctly from the back of the Christmas card he sent me three years ago.

He might not even be there anymore.

He's probably forgotten all about me.

"No," I whisper as I look at my eyes in the rearview mirror. "There's no one to run to. You're on your own. You'll get through this like you get through everything. Dad's death. Mom's suicide. If you can get through that, then you can get through this."

I take a deep breath, drive around for a while, and then park behind a Costco and sleep in my backseat.

———

The next morning, I park across the street from my apartment building and scope it out. I already called in sick to the diner even though I can't afford to, but what else can I do? My uniform is upstairs.

I don't know what I'm hoping to see, but I'll know it when I see it. Crenshaw, the two guys from last night who dragged the body back into the apartment, and two other guys come strutting out of the building around noon. I lower my head and peek over the steering wheel as I watch them get into a car and drive away.

When I'm sure they're gone, I quickly drive over and run into the building. I have to get my stuff.

I manage to not be noticed by anyone as I run up the stairs and down the hallway, but just as I get to my door, Crenshaw's girlfriend walks out of their place.

"Oh fuck!" I gasp when she sees me.

She comes rushing over.

"Get away from me!" I shout as I raise my fists and stare her down. "I'll crack you right in the nose, bitch!"

She shakes her head, looking panicked. "What are you doing here? You have to get out of here. He's looking for you!"

I lower my fists when it's clear she's not looking for a fight.

"What's going to happen if he finds me?" I ask, not really wanting to know the answer to that.

"He's going to do the same thing to you that he did to that guy last night."

"He's going to kill me?"

I swallow hard as she nods. "He's psychotic. You have to leave. They went out for breakfast, so you got about an hour."

"Where I'm supposed to go? I *live* here!"

"Not anymore."

This can't be happening. This *can't* be happening. My hands are shaking as I stare at her in disbelief.

"Is there any place you can go?"

Jack's warm smile pops into my head.

"Anywhere?"

My mouth opens. "Maybe... uh..."

"Then go there," she says as she grabs my shoulders, turns me around, and shoves me. "Now!"

"I just need to grab some... stuff." My stomach sinks when I see my door. Crenshaw kicked it in. The door is open a crack and the doorframe is a mess of splinters and broken shards of wood.

"*No*," I whisper as I push it in and walk inside.

My apartment is in tatters. It's been ransacked. Everything is gone.

"No!" I gasp when I remember my expensive sticker equipment. I run into my spare room and my stomach drops when I see that *everything* is gone. Everything.

I walk around feeling dead inside as I see the life I've built—meager as it was—in shambles. They took it all. They even took my shower curtain. My plant. Even my fridge is gone.

"Crenshaw kicked the door in," the girl says with an apologetic look on her face. "I tried to close the door for you after, but it was all busted up. Half the building took turns robbing you. It was a free-for-all."

"I hate this building."

"You're really going to hate it if you're still here when Crenshaw returns. It's time to go."

I grab a plastic bag off the floor that everyone so generously left me and head over to my bedroom. My dresser is gone but there are a few dirty clothes in my hamper that haven't been touched. I stuff them all into the bag and then hurry into the bathroom. They even took my toothbrush holder. Freaking animals!

I take whatever is left—some deodorant, soap, and a few other things.

I walk back into the main room and spot the photo of my parents on the wall. It's the only one I have.

My heart breaks as I take it off the wall and look at their smiling faces. I'm about two years old in the photo. My father is looking so handsome in his military uniform as he holds me in his muscular arms. What I wouldn't give to feel as safe in his arms right now as I did back then.

The last thing I take is the Christmas card that Jack sent me three years ago. It's in the bottom drawer in the kitchen. It was under the placemats but those are now gone. I take the card and the envelope with his address on the back.

34 Silvergray Mountain, Greene Mountains, Montana.

I run my finger over the faded ink as Crenshaw's girlfriend comes rushing back into my apartment.

"Haven't you done enough?" I ask her. Why can't she just leave me alone?

She shoves a wad of cash into my hand. "Take it."

"How much money is this?" I ask, staring at it in shock.

"Just over five grand. Take it."

"Won't he hurt you when he finds out you stole it?"

She shakes her head. "He won't find out. I've been taking a bit here and there and hiding it in the wall for the day it's my turn to escape."

"Oh," I whisper as I really see her for the first time. She's a victim too. Her eyes are tired and worn out like she's seen way too much trauma for one lifetime. My heart goes out to her.

"I think I'll go live in Cannes," she says more to herself than to me. "I've been learning French."

A flash of optimism burns in her eyes, but it flickers out as quickly as it was sparked.

"He'll probably find me though..."

She catches herself and then shoves the money into my bag. "Be as careful as you can," she warns. "He took your computer and went through your place so he has all of your info. No real names, no social media, no phones."

She grabs my purse, pulls my phone out, and tosses it onto the counter. "He'll track you down with it."

"How the hell am I supposed to do anything without my phone?"

"You're a smart girl," she says as she thrusts my purse back into my hands. "You'll figure it out. Just don't mess up. He will find you if you make a mistake and he *will* come finish the job. He'll send his whole crew after you. He's relentless. He's merciless."

I swallow hard as I stare at the horror in her eyes. "Is that why you haven't left?"

She nods, trying not to cry.

I put my hand on her shoulder and she shakes her tears away, suddenly back to business.

"Go somewhere far," she warns. "Somewhere secluded where he won't be able to track you down. It's the only way."

"Okay," I whisper as I clutch the bag. Everything I have left is in this bag. "You get out too. As soon as you can. Go to Cannes and start over."

A sad look washes over her face. She nods, but I can tell in her defeated eyes that she knows it's just a dream. There will never be a Cannes. There will only be this. A living hell.

"Go!" she says, pushing me to the door. "And good luck."

I take one last look at my ransacked apartment and hurry to my car.

Next stop, The Greene Mountains.

Chapter Two

Jack

"Who will be the next valiant warrior to step into the cage?" Marvin, the owner of the bar bellows into the microphone at the amped-up crowd. It's a full house tonight, packed with the usual rag-tag truckers and tough ranchers, but it looks like we also have a college football team crammed into the seedy bar. They're wearing their team colors—red and white, and are extra rowdy, pounding down beers and pounding on the tables. A few of them are looking like they're ready to get into the cage and pound on something else.

"I'll fight!" a big thick motherfucker shouts in a deep voice as he rises from the table. The football players hoot and holler all around him like a pack of rabid gorillas.

All eyes are on the beast as he charges through the crowd, elbowing and pushing everyone out of his way.

He marches up the steps into the steel cage. The

Olivia T. Turner

plywood floor creaks under his weight. It was painted white years ago, but you can barely see it through all of the red blood stains streaked across it. I was the cause of many of those splatters. It's not my blood though.

"We need a challenger!" Marvin shouts as he scans the suddenly mellowed-out crowd. No one meets his eye as the roided-up Goliath who looks like he was bred to be a line-backer struts around the cage behind him with his arms flexed.

"Who wants some?!" Goliath shouts as he glares at the crowd with crazy eyes. "Come and get it!"

"You going up, Jack?" my buddy Stan asks with a grin.

I sigh as I look at my half-finished beer. "I'm still on my first one."

I like to have at least three in me before I make my way up to the cage.

"You can finish it between rounds," Stan says. "I'll hold it for ya."

I light a smoke and sit back on the stool. We're on the side of the bar next to the wall near the front. The cage is in the back, but this part of the bar is raised so I can see over everyone's heads.

"I want to have a couple of beers first," I say as I take a long drag of my cigarette.

This is the best part of my month and I don't want to rush it. I live for this night. The third Thursday of every month is Fight Night at The Cracked Barrel Saloon. It's the shittiest bar in the state, but it's like a second home to me. On the outskirts of the Greene Mountains, it's normally mostly empty, but on Fight Night... Every meat-head in the area comes flocking to this place looking for glory.

"We're looking for a fierce competitor!" Marvin shouts,

trying to stir up the crowd. "Anyone out there want to test their masculine might?"

A few of the regulars turn and look at me. I just suck down my cigarette smoke and ignore them all.

"Come on!" the roid-head hollers at the top of his lungs as he shakes the cage. The barbed wire wrapped around the top rattles. "Let's go!"

His football team pounds on the tables making a fucking racket. "Pussies! Pussies! Pussies!" They chant, taunting the crowd.

These punks are starting to piss me off.

Marvin's eyes find me in the crowd. He gives me a pleading look. I know Fight Night is what keeps his bar afloat. He makes more in this one night than he does all the other nights of the month combined. If no one is up for a fight, then business is going to suffer as people get bored and stop coming.

"There has to be one champion among you who—"

Goliath grabs the mic out of Marvin's hand and shoves him so hard he flies into the fence and falls to the ground. Stan looks at me over our table. His eyes light up as I crush my cigarette into the ashtray.

"We're on?" he says all giddy as he leaps up from his stool.

"Yeah," I say as I down my beer and then crack open another one. "We're on."

I hand him the bottle and he takes it with an excited little squeal. He's always my corner man, but that just means he holds my beer and my smokes between rounds. When the bell rings after a round, he hands them to me through the fence. That's *if* the bell rings. My fights rarely make it to the end of the first round.

And I'm the only one standing at the end of it.

"I'll fight," I say in a deep voice that cuts through the chatter.

All heads turn to me.

Goliath tosses the mic back at Marvin who's slowly getting up and then pounds his lunchbox of a fist into his palm. He's glaring at me as I make my way down the steps.

"We have a challenger, ladies and gentlemen!" Marvin hollers into the mic even though there are no ladies present tonight (or any other night). "An ex-Navy SEAL and Fight Night legend, Jack 'Watch Your Back' Michaels!"

The regulars cheer. The football players boo and hiss.

The crowd splits in front of me as I make my way up to the cage with Stan following close behind. I pull off my shirt and he takes it.

I can feel the anticipation crackling in the air. The regulars know what I can do. They know that this steroid freak is going to be dragged out of here by his buddies.

They holler as I walk up the steps and step into the cage. The bright fluorescent bulbs hanging from the ceiling light me up and I get a little shot of adrenaline. A little thrill to spice up my rotten life.

Like Marv said, I was a Navy SEAL once. Jumping from one deadly mission to another. Getting shot at, knives thrown at me, grenades launched at my head. It was amazing. Every day was a test of my will. Of my strength. Of my resolve.

I still long for those days. The adventure, the hunt, the thrill of the kill. I'm a warrior with no more war.

And a warrior with no cause is a sad thing. I once had a whole country to protect, but now... Now, I got nothing. I got this. Bare-knuckle brawls in a seedy bar off the highway.

I miss the feeling of making a difference. Of being a protector.

What I really miss is the feeling of sliding that thick black paste on my face before a mission and knowing I'm doing good in the world.

I'm a long way from all that.

"You okay, Marv?" I ask as he shuffles past me.

He gives me a look and shakes his head. "Kick the shit out of him," he whispers before exiting the cage and locking it on the other side.

"Who the fuck is this?" Goliath shouts as he glances back at his buddies. "Grandpa?"

His team bursts out laughing. I grab my lit cigarette through the cage, take a puff, and hand it back to Stan.

This guy is larger than I am and that's not something I say very often. He's got about half a foot and fifty pounds on me.

"You going to stretch first, old man?" Goliath shouts loud enough for the crowd to hear. "A geriatric like you should warm up."

"You are my warm up," I say in a low stone-cold voice.

He scoffs. "We'll see about that."

The beast lunges forward with his big mitts up. He comes at me, throwing a combination of punches—left jab, right jab, left hook. I dodge them all and step out of the way.

My body creaks and groans as I move. I squeeze my hands into fists and keep them by my sides as we circle the cage.

I'm fifty-three years old. My body doesn't move like it used to, but it still moves fast enough.

I'm fighting guys in their twenties. These guys are in their prime. I'm *way* past my prime, but I can still kick the shit out of anyone who steps into the cage with me.

He charges forward with a booming war cry. I plant my legs, rotate my hips, and punch him as hard as I can in the jaw. The war cry turns into a gurgle as his legs wobble and he falls to a knee.

I see his eyes roll back in his head for a second and he looks dazed as his hand hits the matt. I can hit him again—there are no rules on Fight Night, but I hold back my fist and walk over to Stan. He sticks the neck of my beer bottle through the cage and tilts it into my open mouth. I swallow it down and then turn around, watching as Goliath gets to his shaky feet.

He's a tough motherfucker, I'll give him that. I doubt anyone else in the place can take a hit like that and get up after.

A low growl rumbles out of his throat as he glares at me. He reaches up, yanks a section of the barbed wire off the top of the cage, and stares me down as he wraps it around his arm.

That's a new one.

I've never seen a guy do that before.

Blood leaks down his thick forearm as he secures it around his fist. His buddies are going mental—screaming and hollering and having the time of their lives.

I glance at Stan and he gives me a shrug. Next time I'm having my three beers first. It's too early in the night to be dealing with this shit.

I let out a sigh as I cock my fists and get back to work. I head right for him. He swings that barbed wire fist, but I easily duck under it and smash him in the gut with a hard right hook. It takes the air out of his lungs, but he recovers fast and tries to hit me again.

I land three more punches—two in his stomach and one on his cheek.

And then he lands one on me.

Right in the eye. Pain shoots through my brain like a jolt

of lightning. I fly back as my eyes fill with water and my back slams into the cage.

His buddies erupt.

He charges forward and connects again, this time with the barbed wire. I feel skin shred off my face as I'm thrown into the fence. Hot blood drips onto my chest as I take a deep breath, trying to get my brain to stop swirling.

At the last second, it clears. Goliath is charging at me like an angry bull. I duck down, wrap my arms around his legs, and pick him up in a double-leg sweep. I dig my shoulder into his stomach as I slam him into the blood-stained plywood.

He doesn't know what hit him and I take advantage of his confusion to mount up on the bully. I sit on his chest, pinning him down, and then I start raining down bombs on his face.

I'm done showing mercy.

I ground and pound the shit out of him. *Crack. Crack. Crack.*

Pound the pain away.

When I exited the Navy SEALs, my military-issued shrink said that my fighting was a defense mechanism. She said I had to fight to keep myself distracted from the loneliness and the pain.

I say it works and if it ain't broke, don't fix it.

Nothing like a little adrenaline to wash the longing away.

His blood splatters on my chest. I'm covered in it and this guy is still trying to fight back.

One last hard *crack* on his jaw and the last bit of fight leaves his giant body.

I take a deep breath as I look at his bruised and swollen face. There's blood everywhere.

Shit, Jack. What did you do?

I sigh as I get up, my old bones creaking with every movement.

The crowd is going nuts. The football players are silent as they stare at their beaten alpha gorilla in shock.

Marv opens the gate as I arrive at the door. I climb down the steps with a sick feeling in my stomach. This isn't making it better anymore.

The fighting seems to be making the longing worse.

If I don't have this, I don't know what the fuck I'm going to do.

"I said kick his ass," Marv says in a low voice as I pass him, "not murder him."

I ignore him and walk up to Stan who hands me my beer. I down all of it in one gulp.

If fighting won't take the pain away, maybe alcohol will.

The crowd suddenly starts clapping and I turn around, relieved to see the big guy getting up on his own. He's a little wobbly on his feet, but he'll be okay.

Shit, if he's heading to the NFL, what I just did to him is nothing compared to what he's going to encounter every Sunday afternoon.

Hopefully, he's a little less cocky now.

Marv is already hyping the next fight, trying to get two more fighters into the cage.

"Want to stay and go again?" Stan asks, holding a handful of cash. He placed a bet with one of the football players and just made a week's worth of salary.

"Nah," I say with a heaviness weighing down on me. "Let's go watch and drink. You're buying."

I shuffle back to my table, getting all kinds of smacks on my bare shoulder as I go. My face is still bleeding. It's leaking onto my chest.

I ball up my shirt and hold it against my ripped-up cheek when I finally sit down.

There's got to be more to my life than this.

I'm wasting it.

An image of Derek flashes into my mind and I suddenly feel so ashamed. He was a Navy SEAL and he was my best friend. We were so tight.

I would have given my life for him, but that fucking asshole gave his life for me instead. We were in Afghanistan on a secret mission trying to take out a high-profile general of the Taliban. We were always glued to each other in the field. I watched his back and he watched mine. I guess I should have been watching his feet instead...

A grenade rolled into the cave out of nowhere.

He leaped on it before I could...

I sigh as I pop open another beer and down half of it, shivering as I remember the horrible sound, the spray of hot blood, the realization that my best friend in the whole world was suddenly painting the walls of the cave with his insides.

I place the cigarette to my lips with a trembling hand as I remember the funeral. His wife who looked so broken. Those dead eyes...

But it was Derek's little girl that really got me.

Ruby.

She was sixteen at the time, but she looked as wise as an adult with those sparkling blue eyes and soft blonde hair.

I remember the overwhelming feeling of wanting to take her in my arms. To protect her. To shelter her from the evils of the world.

My heart pounds as I recall the way her hand felt when she shook mine. The way she looked at me when I told her that she can always count on me.

It should have been me who got killed in that cave.

I'm the one who should be a distant memory and Derek should be the one still here. He should be taking care of his girl. He should be her protector.

I sigh as I crush my cigarette into the ashtray.

The longing becomes unbearable. The pain too much.

"I'm gonna go again," I tell Stan as the need to punch and get punched takes over. "One more fight."

Stan leaps up and waves to Marvin who's trying to get another fighter in.

"Jack wants to go again!"

The whole crowd cheers, even the football players. Even Goliath who is holding a cold bottle of beer against his swollen face while drinking another one.

The only one who doesn't look excited is the poor fuck who's already in the cage.

I'll go easy on him.

Probably.

Chapter Three

Jack

My head is still ringing from that linebacker's fat knuckles on the drive home. I groan as I turn onto my steep street, gunning it up the mountain as my bones ache and my head throbs.

It's after three in the morning. It's pitch black up here, except for whatever my headlights touch.

I ended up fighting three guys and I laid all of them out.

On the way to my truck, four drunk fuckers tried to start shit in the parking lot with me, but they quickly dispersed once I grabbed their leader by the throat and tossed his ass onto the concrete.

All in all, it was a good night.

My pulse slows as I slide a cigarette out of my pack and put it to my cracked bloody lips. I light it and inhale deep, watching as the swirling smoke lit up by the blue lights on my dashboard fills the interior of my truck.

I imagine the smoke filling my insides which always feel so damn hollow, and then I exhale long and slow.

My truck approaches the bend up ahead with the steep cliff a few feet from the dirt road.

After every Fight Night I imagine gunning the engine and flying off it. Ending the pain. Going out in a fiery explosion of glory.

Ah, who am I kidding? There would be no glory. Just an old sad dead man in the woods with no one to grieve him. No one to even notice he was gone.

My foot gets heavy on the gas. The truck speeds up. My pulse races.

I squeeze the steering wheel and grit my teeth, going faster, faster...

"Fuck it," I mutter as I yank the wheel at the last moment. My tires skid through the dirt, launching rocks and pebbles over the cliff before they catch and I whip around the bend.

I shake my head—heart pounding—as I continue driving up to my house.

This mountain has hardly anyone on it. Only six houses scattered around the huge base and the one higher up near the summit, which is mine.

"What the fuck is this?" I whisper when I pull into my long driveway and spot an old beaten-up car parked in it. Washington plates.

Robbers. Criminals from the city. They must have come up here thinking we're easy prey.

Boy, did these fuckers pick the wrong house.

I'm flushed with heat as I squeeze the wheel, getting excited for round two.

And that's when I see her.

She walks into the shine of my headlights, waving shyly.

The anger vanishes. My mouth drops. My heart stops.

I slowly hit the brake and put my truck into park as I watch her with my body humming.

It's her.

It's Ruby.

I'd recognize those beautiful blue eyes and that shy innocent smile anywhere.

What is she doing here? What is happening?

The only thought that makes sense is that I must have missed the turn. I must have flown off the edge of the cliff and this is heaven right here.

She's my angel come to greet me.

I stare at her in awe.

But then my hand drops down and the glowing cherry of my cigarette burns my thigh. The pain makes me realize that this is actually happening. This is real.

I swallow hard, crush the cigarette in the ashtray on my dashboard, and step out of the car with goosebumps sliding along the back of my neck.

I can't stop staring at her. I can't take my eyes off her angelic face.

"Ruby?" I ask in a low shaky voice. "Is that you?"

"Hi, Jack," she says, suddenly struggling to hold back tears. Her chin quivers and I slam the door of my truck and race over.

"Come here," I say as I swallow her in my big arms, holding her against my chest. I wonder if she can feel how hard my heart is pounding. "You're safe now, baby girl. You're with me."

Her body shakes and she lets out a deep sob, melting into my embrace as I hold her like I'm never going to let her go.

"I'm sorry," she says, shaking her head and wiping her

cheeks when she finally pulls away. "It's the first time I cried... I just... I saw you and it all came gushing out."

I let her go, but my hands are trembling with the need to hold her again. My whole body is aching.

"Are you okay?" I ask her, not knowing what I'm going to do if she's not. "What happened?"

That's when she notices my face. "Are *you* okay?" she asks with a gasp. "What happened to your face?"

She reaches for my cheek but I flinch away from her touch. Shame hits me harder than Goliath ever could. This is what her father gave her life for.

This monstrosity of a life.

Drinking, smoking, fighting—She had to grow up without a father for *this*.

"I... got into a car accident."

My cheeks burn with shame. I hate myself. This is a new fucking low.

She looks at my truck—the headlights still burning—and scrunches her forehead up in confusion when she sees that it's in perfect condition.

"It was at work."

I hate myself for lying to her, but I just can't let her know how much of a fuck up I am. How pathetic I've become.

"What happened?" I ask again. "Are you in danger?"

She sucks in a long breath and then looks up at me. "Can we go inside?"

"Of course," I tell her as I jump into action. I hurry back to my truck and turn the engine off.

"Do you have any bags?" I ask as she lingers by her car.

"Just one," she says before opening the passenger door and pulling out a plastic bag full of stuff. "It's all I have left."

I have a million questions for her, but first, I have to get her inside. I open the front door and let her go in.

"Can I use the bathroom?" she asks in a soft voice.

"Of course. Over here."

She closes the door and I burst into action, racing around my house in a flurry, cleaning faster than anyone has ever cleaned before. Dirty dishes get shoved into the dishwasher, unwashed clothes get thrown into my closet, empty bottles get tossed into the recycling bin, and overflowing ashtrays get launched outside into the back. The place looks better by the time she comes out. Not great, but decent.

"Are you hungry? Thirsty?" I ask when she makes her way into the kitchen, nervously rubbing her slender thighs.

I yank the fridge open and curse under my breath when I see beer, beer, and more beer. There's not much in the way of food. I have a few frozen elk steaks in the freezer in the basement, but I'm not about to offer her that.

"I'd love a beer," she says with a tired sigh. "If you have one."

"That I have," I say, thankful to give her what she needs. I pull out a beer, open it, and hand it to her.

"Thanks, Jack," she whispers as she takes it. Her finger grazes mine and my whole body shivers.

I watch her soft pink lips wrap around the opening of the bottle. I swallow hard as my heart thumps harder at the beautiful sight.

This is Derek's daughter, I have to remind myself. I tear my eyes away from her as self-loathing washes over me. If anyone on the planet is off-limits, it's her.

"Come," I say, ushering her to the sofas. "Sit."

She sits on one and I sit on the other, keeping the coffee table between us. I don't quite trust myself right now.

I give her a moment, letting her have a few sips as she gets her thoughts together.

"I'm sorry to barge in on you like this," she says as she looks at the beer bottle in her hands.

"Not at all," I quickly tell her. "You're always welcome here, Ruby."

She smiles sadly at me. "Thank you. I remember what you told me... at my dad's funeral. I had nowhere else to go, so..."

A fresh wave of tears hits her beautiful blue eyes. I squeeze my hand into a fist as I struggle to keep my ass planted on the couch. My whole body is screaming at me to go to her, but my conscience—what little of it is left—is telling me not to fucking move.

"Tell me what happened," I whisper in a firm voice. "Tell me everything."

My body stiffens and my blood runs cold as she tells me how she witnessed a murder and then ran from the killer. I'm breathing heavily with rage filling every cell in my body as she tells me how she slept behind a dumpster, how she was robbed, how they took everything from her.

I want to burn down the world to keep her safe. I want to find every last one of those fucking punks and show them the meaning of hell.

I'm struggling to keep it together by the time she's finished.

"I just need a place to stay for a few days," she says, "while I figure out what to do."

She's never leaving.

"Of course. As long as you need."

Those shiny blue eyes fill with gratitude as she watches me. "Thank you, Jack."

"I'm glad you came to me, Ruby. I didn't know you were living all alone in the city." It makes me all tight and shaky to know she's been on her own, surrounded by all those freaks, perverts, and animals. The thought of her so vulnerable in a human circus like that... Fuck, I don't even want to think about it.

"How come you're not living with your mother?"

Her eyes dart up to mine. "You don't know?"

My body gets so heavy it feels like I'm being pulled into the couch. "Know what?"

"Mom..." She takes a deep breath as my chest tightens. "Mom committed suicide."

"*What...?* When?"

"About three years ago."

The heaviness turns to numbness. Angela is dead?

She always looked so happy whenever she was on Derek's arm. I was the best man at their wedding. I thought they were the luckiest two people in the world whenever I saw how they looked at one another.

The sadness is crippling. Why is this world so fucking cruel? My eyes get all hot and watery, my throat scratchy as it hits.

"You've been on your own... Since you were *nineteen*?"

Her mouth forms a straight line as she shrugs.

I dart around the table and sit beside her, grabbing her hands and squeezing them too hard as tears leak out of my eyes. "I'm so sorry, Ruby," I say, desperately wishing I could take the years back. "I didn't know... I would have helped you. I would have gotten you... I..."

I drop my head in shame. Is there anything in my life I haven't fucked up?

Maybe if I had kept in touch with Angela, maybe if I... *Fuck.* It was always too hard. It was easier to drown out the memory of Derek in a bottle than it was to face it. It was easier to hide up here than it was to stay and take care of his family.

33

"It's okay," she whispers as she gently touches my face. She pulls my head back up until I'm looking into her watery eyes. "You're here now. You're helping me now."

I swallow hard as I stare at her beautiful face through my blurry vision. She's stunning.

She's the most magnificent thing I've ever seen.

After all the shit she's been through, she still manages to have an angelic wholesome way about her. The way she's looking up at me... It's so innocent. So pure.

Those plump lips...

That sultry body...

She has no idea how tempting she is.

I squeeze my eyes shut and curse myself out.

This is not the way to repay your best friend. He gave the ultimate sacrifice for you and here you are lusting after his daughter like a creep when she needs your help.

I grit my teeth as my heart pounds with self-loathing.

You're a fucking monster. You're as bad as the guys who took everything from her. Even worse since she trusts you.

I dart up off the couch and open my eyes. I stare at the floor, not trusting myself to look at the devil's temptation in front of me.

"You must be tired," I say in a cracked shaky voice. "I'll run you a bath and set you up in the spare bedroom. The mattress is decent. I don't think it's ever been used so..."

She takes my hand. Her skin is so fucking soft.

I try to keep my eyes off her, but they won't fucking listen. My heart squeezes as I stare down at her in awe. She's looking up at me with so much trust in those tear-stained blue eyes. If only she knew what I was thinking... She'd be sprinting back to her car and racing down the mountain to get away from me.

"Thank you, Jack. I don't know what I'd do without you."

"You've been doing just fine without me all this time," I say, still hating that I wasn't there for her. "You would have figured something out. You're the strongest person I know, Ruby. With all you've been through... I know Navy SEALs who couldn't have made it through what you have."

She smiles sadly at me.

Those beautiful eyes drop to my hand that she's still holding. She runs her thumb over my bruised knuckles and then looks back up at me.

"Car accident?"

I pull my hand away and take a deep breath. "I'll get that bath going."

My breath is lodged in my chest until I'm in the bathroom with the door closed. I turn the bath on and then drop to the floor, not quite knowing what hit me.

I hang my head between my legs as so many conflicting thoughts spiral through my head like a tornado.

I want her. I need her.

And I hate that I fucking do.

She's just a kid, a part of me says.

She's not a kid anymore, another darker part of me answers.

The hot water fills the tub as I drop my head into my hands, angrier at Derek than I've ever been.

Why? I ask him as my veins flow with fury. *Why didn't you let me die?*

You could have been here for her.

Instead, she has *me*.

And what do I have to offer this angel?

What good is still left in a broken man like me?

Chapter Four

Jack

She's in the bath...

"Don't think about it," I mutter to myself as I storm into the kitchen. "Don't you even fucking think about it."

I head right for the cupboard where I store my liquor. I had my last sip of alcohol at the bar.

I'll never touch the poison again.

I yank off the cork of my half-empty bottle of Scotch and turn it upside down in the sink. The Whiskey goes next. Then the Vodka. Then the Tequila.

Glug, glug glug... All of them, down the drain.

I grit my teeth as I watch the dark liquid circle the drain before disappearing down it.

"I'll never drink another drop as long as I have an angel to protect," I whisper, vowing it to her, to the heavens, and to myself. I'm not going near the stuff ever again.

Everything goes. Rum, Gin, Beer—even the Peppermint Schnapps that someone gave me at Christmas a few years ago. I gather all of the empty bottles and cans in a garbage bag, carry them outside, and dump them into the recycling bin.

There's zero hesitation. No doubts at all.

I have Ruby now. I don't need anything else.

My cigarettes go next. I grab the packs I have, open them all, and then run them under water as I think of Ruby's beautiful blue eyes. I shiver, remembering the way she was looking at me with such trust and admiration.

I don't deserve her respect, but I'm committed to earning it one day. This is just a start.

I toss the soggy tobacco into the garbage, tie it up, and bring it to the garbage bin outside.

Once it's in, I stand back and have a tremor of doubt. *Can I do this?*

"You can do anything," I whisper to myself. "You got through SEAL training and that's the toughest test in the world. You've been through hell in jungles, deserts, and war-torn cities. You can do this. You *will* do this, for her."

I steel my nerves, trying to scrounge up some of that bold macho fortitude that came so easily in my twenties. I squeeze my arms, feeling some of that masculine tenacity returning into my hard biceps and flexed shoulders.

I'm not going to fail. I'm not going to let her down.

I'll be the man that Ruby deserves and the sharp proficient protector she needs.

Every time I crave a drink, I'll do fifty push-ups. Every time I want to light a smoke, I'll do fifty burpees.

I'll let my cravings be my trainer. I'll turn my weaknesses into physical strength.

With my mind set, I head back inside.

My mother always said I was too stubborn for my own good. She said that once I had my mind set on something, the entire US military couldn't stand in my way.

Well, my mind is set on this.

I'll stay clean for Ruby. I'll try every day to be worthy of the way she was looking at me.

The bath is draining when I walk back into the house.

My chest gets all tight when I hear the door open and those soft footsteps coming down the hall.

"Jesus..." I whisper when I see her in the T-shirt I gave her to sleep in. It's green army camouflage, but it's doing nothing to hide her curves. I swallow hard when I see the way her round breasts are pushing out against it, the shape of her firm nipples in view. I drop my eyes to the ground, not wanting to tempt the hungry beast inside me.

But even as I look away, I can still see the image of her bountiful chest burning in my brain.

"Thanks for the shirt," she says as I squeeze my hands into fists at my side. "They took all of my pajamas."

I'm shaky all over as I force my eyes up to hers. Her blonde hair is wet and she's no longer wearing any makeup. I suck in a sharp breath when I see how beautiful she is. She's stunning.

The ultimate temptation.

I could just go to her now, pull that shirt off her head, and she'd be completely naked and at my mercy.

Fuck, I curse myself as I tear my eyes off her.

If my best friend could hear the thoughts in my head right now... He'd probably come back to life just to end mine.

"I'm going to bed," she says in that soft innocent voice that's like candy to my ears.

My eyes dart back to her as she makes her way over. My

shirt ends halfway up her thighs and those long bare legs look so enticing it's hard to breathe. Even her feet are a work of art—long slender arches with perfect little pink toes. I could spend hours massaging them without wanting to stop.

She stops in front of me and a whiff of coconut soap fills my lungs. She smells so good. So fresh and pure. My mouth waters as I look down into her eyes.

"Thank you for everything, Jack," she whispers. "I don't know what I'd do without you."

That tiny hand touches my chest as she rises on her toes to kiss my cheek. Her soft wet lips touch my stubbled skin and I fight back every intense urge ripping through my body.

It takes everything I have to keep my hands to myself.

She drops back down onto her heels and smiles shyly at me before tucking a strand of damp hair behind her ear and turning away.

My eyes are on those long gorgeous legs and on her round ass as I watch her walk back down the hall. She disappears from view and my legs buckle.

I grab onto a kitchen chair and slump down onto it with my body aching.

I have the devil's temptation in my house and I can't let myself indulge.

This is going to be torture.

Chapter Five

Ruby

I pull the warm blankets up to my heart and cuddle them as I moan on the soft pillow. I don't remember ever feeling more safe and secure than I do right now.

I know that Jack will look out for me. I know I'm in good hands.

He might be a little rough around the edges, but he's going to look out for my safety. Crenshaw won't stand a chance against a warrior like him.

A warm fluttering ripples through my chest as I think about him. The way he was looking at me with those light brown eyes, so full of... something. I don't know what it was, but it's making the heat in my chest flow down between my legs as I recall the intensity of it.

I've had a crush on him since I was a kid.

Even before I hit puberty, I remember pulling out my parents' wedding album just to gaze at the pictures of Jack in his gray suit. His hair was shorter back then and he was clean-shaven, but I like the mountain man look he's rocking now. It suits him well with the long silver fox hair and thick masculine beard. He's the most manly man I've ever seen.

I can imagine Crenshaw stepping up to a man like Jack and trying to intimidate him. Crenshaw is nothing but a bully, whereas Jack is a true warrior. He wouldn't be intimidated. He'd smack him down with those huge hands and send him fleeing with his tail between his legs.

I turn around in bed with a moan and look at the closed door, wishing he'd come in. I'm not sure what I want, but I know I want to be near him. I want him to lay down next to me and wrap those big strong protective arms around me. I want to feel his hands on me, his hot breath on me. I want to feel his heart pounding against my back and his hard desire pressed against me.

I want to know that he wants me as much as I want him.

He's the only man I've ever wanted.

The only one who's lit my fire.

But I know it's never going to happen. He's my father's best friend.

He probably sees me as a dumb kid who screwed up and got herself into trouble.

I just hope he thinks I'm not a nuisance for being here.

I'll have to figure this out quickly and find a new place to stay before I annoy him too much. Being a burden to him is the last thing in the world I want to be.

I'm staring at the faint crack of light at the bottom of the door when a shadow suddenly appears.

I hold my breath as I wait for the door handle to turn.

Is he going to come in?

I can't breathe as I wait... and wait...

Finally, the shadow disappears and I'm left all alone once more.

What was I thinking? That he actually wanted me?

I let out the long breath I was holding and cling to the blankets as the heat and desire flooding my body goes cold.

At least I have his shirt to sleep in. At least that part of him is touching my body.

It's not even close to what I want, but I'll take what little part of him I can get.

Chapter Six

Ruby

It's almost noon by the time I wake up. I stretch out in bed with a blissful moan, feeling so content after my good night's sleep. There's nothing like waking up refreshed after being exhausted for days.

I use the ensuite bathroom to wash up and put on the nicest outfit I have left—my favorite pair of jeans and an old Beastie Boys T-shirt.

I'm still yawning and rubbing my heavy eyes when I walk down the hall and see Jack at the stove. There are grocery bags everywhere and he's cooking up a feast.

"Did you go grocery shopping?" I ask as I take a seat at the granite island.

"I didn't know what you like," he says as he starts the pot of coffee, "so, I got everything."

I laugh. "I can see that. You didn't have to do all of that on my account."

He smiles shyly. "The fridge was pretty empty last night and you look like you needed a good meal, so... It's nothing."

I watch as he moves around the kitchen, flipping eggs and putting crusty bread into the toaster. He moves quick and lithe for someone so big and muscular. Each movement is as graceful and agile as a large predator cat. It's unreal.

He's looking more put together today with a nice pair of jeans and a light blue collared shirt. The sleeves are rolled up his thick forearms and I swallow hard when I see the veins running up them. His long salt and pepper hair is pulled back nicely, but his face is still bruised and cut up. The bruise around his eye has turned a dark shade of purple.

"Can I help?"

"I got it," he says with a smile. "I just want you to relax."

I don't think anyone has ever said that to me before. I'm always at work, so I'm used to bosses barking at me non-stop to get moving. Relaxing is a nice change.

"What are you making?" I ask as he pulls out a knife and an avocado.

"The guy at the grocery store said your generation loves avocado toast. Is that true? I didn't know what it was so I looked it up."

I can't help but smile as I picture this manly man in the grocery store googling avocado toast for me.

"I've never had it, but I'm sure it's going to be amazing."

He smiles gratefully at me and then starts slicing up the avocado. My eyes drop to his big hands and that warmth from last night comes flooding back into my body. He handles the knife like a master chef, slicing and chopping with speed and ease. I wonder if he learned how to handle a knife like that in culinary school or in the Navy SEALs, but I'm not about to ask.

"How did you know where to find me?" he asks as he washes the knife.

"I kept the Christmas card you sent," I tell him, feeling embarrassed that I kept a Christmas card for three years. Only hoarders or obsessed psychos would do something like that. "It was on the envelope."

"I looked up your address," he says as he starts cutting up some kiwi. "I hope you don't mind."

"Not at all," I quickly say. "I thought it was very sweet."

He looks up at me and our eyes meet. My skin tingles as the air between that intense eye contact charges with electric heat.

I'm blushing when he pulls away.

I was so touched to receive that card. It was the only one I got that year and I had spent Christmas all alone. It was so nice to know that someone out there was thinking of me. It kept me going through the rough holidays.

The coffee maker beeps and I get up to get a mug. "Do you want some coffee?"

"I'd love some," he says as he cuts some ripe mangoes. "Black."

He puts the meal together and we sit at the table with a feast of scrambled eggs, croissants, breakfast potatoes, fresh fruit, and avocado toast.

I haven't eaten like this in years. In fact, this is the first time since my mother died that someone cooked me a meal. I'm always grabbing some extra food from the diner and microwaving it when I get home. I never eat like this.

"It's so beautiful up here," I say as I gaze out the giant windows. Jack has a spectacular view of the mountains that go on forever. It feels like I'm in an untouched part of the world. "I didn't get to see it last night. I only arrived after dark."

"I'm sorry I wasn't around," he says, looking upset at himself.

I put my hand on his and he stills. "You didn't know I was going to show up out of the blue. You don't have to apologize."

He doesn't look like he agrees.

"Plus, you were busy with your... accident."

I run my thumb over his bruised knuckles, hoping he's okay.

He takes a deep breath and looks at me. "It wasn't an accident," he says in a low voice. "I don't want to lie to you, Ruby. I'll never lie to you again. I was competing in a cage match."

"A *cage* match?"

He sighs. "There's a bar that throws them once a month. I go because, well... I don't know. It makes me feel... something."

"You don't have to explain, Jack," I tell him. "You're like my father. You were both born warriors. It must be hard when there's nothing to fight for."

"There wasn't," he says in a low possessive tone as he watches me. "But there is now."

My body shivers with the way he's looking at me. If he keeps looking at me like that, I might do something crazy like kiss him. I turn away before my body takes over and I do something stupid like that. He'd probably laugh at me and send me packing.

"Are those...? Old photos?" I ask, staring at the shoebox on the coffee table in shock.

"Yeah," he says as he gets up and grabs them off the table. "I figured you'd like to see them."

My heart is frozen as he returns with the box. I only have one photo of my parents and it's always been such a sore spot with me. I had put my mother's collection in a storage unit with some of her other stuff after she died, but there was a flash flood out of nowhere and they all got ruined.

My hands are trembling as I go through the box, picking up thick stacks of photos and cycling through them.

Most are of Jack in his youth, and these are just as interesting. I try not to linger too long on the photos of him in his twenties—Navy uniform, bright brown eyes, gorgeous smile. He's shirtless in some of them with his perfect physique and shredded abs. I'll have to come back to these later and take a longer look while he's busy in the shower. I might even have to sneak some of them when I leave.

"Oh wow," I whisper when I spot a photo of Jack and my dad. They're in their Navy SEAL gear in some jungle. My father looks just how I remembered him. Tears fill my eyes as I stare at his gorgeous smiling face.

He has his arm on Jack's shoulders, looking so carefree and happy.

"That was the day he found out your mom was pregnant," Jack says. "He couldn't wipe that smile off his face."

I graze my finger over his face, smiling through my tears as I picture him finding out that he was going to be a father.

"Do you miss him?" I ask.

Jack looks like he's holding back tears. "All the time."

I turn back to the photo and this time I look at Jack. He's so handsome in the picture, but I much prefer the older version in front of me. This young Jack may have the youthful energy and exuberance, but he's missing the wisdom and softness behind those brown eyes that my Jack has.

"I always felt so... horrible, about what happened," he says. "I want you to know, Ruby, that I would change spots with him if I could. I wish it would have been me who died and then you'd still have your father."

"Don't say that ever again," I say as I look at his blurry face. I wipe the tears from my eyes and sniff. "He was being what he was born to be—A hero."

Jack lets out a long sigh. "He was definitely a hero."

"I'm glad you're here with me right now," I say as I touch his big hand. "I'm glad he saved you."

We look at each other for a long moment and then a picture of my mother catches my eye. I grab it out of the box and smile when I see her in her wedding dress. It must be the end of the night because she looks tipsy as hell.

More happy tears flood my eyes as I start cycling through the photos. They're all photos of the wedding, but they're not the staged, everybody-standing-still-for-the-photographer kind of photos. These are the backstage, unrestricted access shots.

I laugh when I see a photo of my mom and dad taking a shot. More pictures are of them dancing on the dance floor, kissing at the head table, my mom sleeping on my dad's shoulder at the end of the night. He looks so happy as he kisses her head.

"These are amazing," I say as I cycle through them again. "I've never seen anything like these before. What I wouldn't give to go back in time and be a fly on the wall. To see them so young, so happy, so..."

It's so overwhelming. The emotions get the better of me and I start crying for real.

Jack gets up and stands behind me. He wraps his big warm arms around me and holds me as I cry. "It's okay, baby girl," he whispers. "Wherever they are, they're thinking of you."

I put my hand on his forearm and take a deep breath, trying to get a hold of myself.

"You can take those with you," he whispers. "I want you to have them."

I shouldn't accept such a precious gift, but I do. "Thank you," I whisper back. "Thank you for everything, Jack."

"Anything for you, baby girl," he says as he gives me one more hug before letting go. "Anything for you."

Chapter Seven

Ruby

After the emotional morning, we head outside and have some fun.

Jack takes me on a breathtaking hike. Literally. The mountain is so steep and he moves so fast that I'm huffing and puffing by the time we get to the top.

"What do you think?" he asks with a grin when we arrive at the summit. I spin around, taking in miles of gorgeous mountains, the picturesque little town below, the trees, the rivers, the lakes—it's untouched wilderness and it's fucking perfect.

I haven't been in a natural wonderland like this since I was a kid. It warms my soul and fills my heart. I can already feel the trauma and horror of what happened slipping away like it was all a bad dream. I feel lighter and more at ease.

No stress from work and the constant grind. I've needed a vacation for so long. I may only be hiding out and it's going to be a lot more stressful when I have to eventually remerge into society worse off than I was before—no job, no more sticker company, no apartment, no stuff—but I'm going to take what I can get. I decide to treat it like a vacation and give myself a well-deserved break.

"I love it out here," I say as I watch a chipmunk scurry over Jack's shoe and disappear into the bush. "I'd love to move out here when I retire one day. *If* I ever retire."

"Why wait?"

I look at him and he shrugs shyly. "I mean, why not move now? The city isn't a safe place for you and you said it yourself that you're probably going to lose your job at the diner and the Chinese restaurant."

"Don't remind me," I mutter. Neither of my two bosses are the forgiving type and they're not going to want to hear any excuses about why I disappeared without any warning. I still haven't called either of them. I should do that when I get back to Jack's place.

"It would be nice," I say, letting myself indulge in the fantasy a bit. Jogging through the mountains in the morning, the safety of the town, the friendly people, and of course, being close to Jack. Maybe I can find a place that's hiring and rent a spare room out over someone's garage or something like that. I can save up to repurchase the equipment that was stolen and restart my sticker empire again.

"Good, so it's settled," Jack says in a firm voice. "You're staying."

I look at him with a grin. "I didn't say that..."

He lets out a *humph* as his protective eyes narrow on me. "We'll see. Come on, let's go back down. There's more I want to show you."

We head down the trail, but I keep looking at Jack from the corner of my eye. He's wearing a green tank top and I can't seem to take my eyes off of his giant arms and broad shoulders. This man is a beast in the best possible way.

I just wish we weren't so far apart in age. It doesn't bother me at all—I love his mature age, it's so sexy—but I know he still sees me as his best friend's little kid. I wonder if I can ever shake off that image he has of me.

Or, if I'm going to be stuck in the friend zone forever.

———

"Like this?" I ask Jack as I hold up the throwing ax.

He steps behind me, dwarfing me with his huge muscular frame. "Yeah," he says as he slides his big hand along my arm, lining my wrist up with the bullseye. "Release it like I showed you. When it's perpendicular to your arm."

I take a deep breath as he steps back. It's hard to focus on anything when he's around, let alone throwing a freaking ax at a huge wooden target.

He told me he liked to throw axes for fun, and I said I wanted to try. I meant in some hypothetical future, not right now, but hey, I guess you have to do outdoorsy stuff like this once in a while when you have a crush on a big hulking mountain man.

"Keep your eye on the bullseye," he says as I pull my arm back.

I'm going to embarrass myself, I just know it. This thing is not going anywhere near that bullseye.

I take a deep breath and launch it just like he showed me, but it sails wide to the right—way worse than I thought —and sinks into the trunk of a harmless tree standing behind the target.

"Oh no!" I gasp, my hands flying to my mouth. "Sorry, tree!"

Jack chuckles as he walks over. "Pretty good for a first try."

"Really?" I ask in a sarcastic tone. "You're seriously going to stand there and tell me that was *good?!*"

He laughs harder. "Maybe not. Let's try again."

"No way," I say, crossing my arms over my chest when he tries to hand me another ax. "I'm done with throwing axes in the middle of the wilderness. How about you take me into that cute little town I passed and you can show me around?"

"Like a date?" he asks. "Sorry. I didn't mean—"

"Yeah," I say, a huge smile building on my face. "Like a date."

————

"You're not drinking?" I ask after the bartender leaves. I ordered a pint of red beer, but Jack only ordered a soft drink.

"No," he says with a smile and a shake of his head. "I don't drink anymore."

"Oh," I say, suddenly feeling bad that I suggested we go to a bar. "We can leave if you're uncomfortable or if you'd rather do something else."

He puts his big hand on mine, swallowing it completely. "It's okay, Ruby. I don't need alcohol when I have you."

My cheeks start to blush, so I turn away before he sees the red flooding into them. This bar is so cute. It's called Cliffside Tavern and seems to be the hot spot in the Greene Mountains. At least it is tonight. The place is packed and we were lucky to snag two bar stools at the end of the bar when a couple suddenly got up.

It seems like the entire place is made of wood, but it's designed in a way to make it look both warm and stylish at the same time. Old classic rock blasts through the speakers and everyone on the dance floor is dancing to Bryan Adam's *Summer Of '69*.

"Were you alive in 1969?" I ask him with a grin.

He laughs. "No, but I came close. I was born in 1970. You?"

I don't want to tell him that I was born in 2001. It's just going to remind him how young I am compared to him. "No, I wasn't alive in '69 either."

He chuckles as he watches me. "Yeah, I didn't think so."

A big burly guy squeezes beside me to get a drink and Jack's light brown eyes narrow on him. He drapes his arm on the back of my stool protectively until the guy is gone.

"So, you work in construction?" I ask him, wanting to know every detail about this man's life. He mentioned it before but didn't go into specifics. I'm so curious about him, but he doesn't seem to volunteer much information. He's a puzzle that I'm committed to solving.

"When I feel like it," he says as the bartender returns with our drinks. Jack quickly pays him before I can even reach for my purse. "My buddy Stan has a construction company and I help him out from time to time when he's short on guys. I don't need the money, but it's fun once in a while. I work outside, get some good exercise, and his crew has some funny guys on it that are always good for a laugh. I'm semi-retired, I guess."

Semi-retired sounds like a dream.

"And what about you?" he asks. "You work in a diner?"

"*Worked* in a diner," I say with a sad laugh. "I don't

think they'll take me back, but the good thing about working in diners is that there's always another one around the corner to apply to."

"You don't seem to like it..."

I sigh as I wrap my hands around the cold mug. "I'd rather be working on my business, but it's okay."

"What's your business?"

I tell him all about my sticker company and how I saved up to buy all of the specialized equipment and how exciting it was when I got my first few orders. I ramble on about all of the platforms, my website, the orders, and everything else. He just calmly listens to everything I have to say, asking thoughtful questions and encouraging me to go on.

"I'm sorry," I say when I catch myself. "I can go on about this forever. Just stop me next time when I get carried away talking about it. I don't want to bore you."

"You're not boring me at all," he says with a bit of fierceness in his tone. "I love hearing you talk about your passion. Your face lights up. It's beautiful to watch. I could listen to you talk about it for hours."

"Oh," I say, looking down at my beer as my heart pounds a little harder. I wasn't expecting that.

"Did all of your equipment get...?"

He doesn't want to say the word. That's okay, because I don't want to hear it.

"Yeah," I say with a sigh. "It's all gone."

He puts a comforting hand on my shoulder and his touch ignites something within me. Heated desire billows out from that hand and blossoms in my chest.

My crush on Mr. Jack Michaels is stronger than ever.

We talk for hours at the bar about everything and anything. By the time I've finished my second beer, we're both turned on our stools and facing each other with my knees tucked between his long muscular legs.

"I can't believe you haven't seen Game of Thrones," I say as I lean in extra close, getting a nice delicious whiff of his masculine scent. He smells like a foresty aftershave. The beer is making me a little braver than normal, so I put my hand on his muscular thigh as I lean in, using the loud music as an excuse to get in nice and close.

He doesn't seem to mind.

"I barely watch any TV," he says as he leans in close. "I prefer to read."

"I love books," I say with a flirty grin. "My favorite is Lolita. Ever heard of it?"

He inhales deeply as he looks at me with a hunger in those burning brown eyes. The air thickens all around us as our lustful eyes say what we're unable to.

"Ruby, I—"

"Ruby!" some girl squeals, yanking me out of this beautiful little bubble I'm hiding out in with Jack. "I thought that was you!"

It's a girl I went to high school with. We had some of the same friends but were never that close. Still, it's good to see her even though this is horrible timing.

"Hey, Michele!" I say with a big smile. "What are you doing here?!"

She comes over and kisses me on both cheeks. She smiles politely at Jack, but then does a double-take when she sees how big he is.

"I'm here on vacation," she shouts over the music. "With my fiancée."

"I didn't know you were getting married!"

"He just proposed yesterday!" she says, giddy with excitement as she shows me the ring. "He took me on this beautiful hike to a waterfall and then got down on one knee and asked. Can you believe it?! I'm getting married!"

"It's beautiful," I say, making a big fuss over the ring.

"That's him. His name is Doug." She points to a guy across the bar at a high table for two. The guy waves with an awkward smile on his face.

"That's amazing!" I tell her. "Congratulations, I'm *so* happy for you!"

"You're going to have to come to the wedding," she says. "Let me get your number."

I glance at Jack as she pulls out her phone. It's nice to see an old friend, but I just wish she'd leave. I want to be alone with him again.

I give her my number and then she insists on taking a selfie together.

"No one is going to believe I ran into you in this tiny town," she says as she holds up the phone and snaps a few pics.

I'm smiling, but my mind is on Jack. I want to be alone with him. Not just in this bar... I want it to be just us. With no one around to see what we do.

"I should get back to my *fiancée*," she says with a giddy laugh. "I'll be in touch, Ruby. We'll grab some coffee or something."

"Definitely!"

She quickly looks Jack over, smiling politely, and then leaves.

I take a breath of relief when she's finally gone.

"Want to get out of here?" I ask Jack, leaning in nice and close.

He looks down at me with a look that gives me warm shivers.

"Yeah. Let's go."

Chapter Eight

Jack

I'm squeezing the steering wheel and trying to only focus on my breathing as I drive down Main Street. I'm keeping my eyes straight ahead and not on the sexy-as-hell, slightly tipsy girl in my passenger seat who's staring at me with those glossy, aroused-filled eyes. Her hair has come down in a bit of a mess, but the tousled look is just turning me on even more.

And that mouth... those lips... *fuck*. They're the color of cherries, but they look even sweeter.

You can't, I remind myself. *She's off-limits.*

"Imagine we were the same age," she says in that sweet voice that makes the tiny hairs on the back of my neck rise. "Do you think we'd, you know..."

I look at her and she smiles shyly.

"...be interested in each other?"

I swallow hard as I turn back to the road, not knowing what to say. I don't care what age she is. Between eighteen and a hundred, I'd be interested in this goddess.

How could I not be? She's perfect in every way.

This day has been the best one in memory. It's the first day without a looming sense of doom hovering over my head. I was cloaked in darkness and she's a new light shining in.

"But we're not the same age," I whisper. "I'm old enough to be your dad."

"It's called imagination, Jack," she says with a playful grin. "Pick a number in the middle. Imagine we were both thirty-seven years old."

I was in Afghanistan hunting down high-ranking members of the Taliban when I was thirty-seven. I push that away and picture myself with an older version of Ruby.

"Okay."

"Now, imagine you're hanging out in a coffee shop," she says, painting the mental picture. "It's raining and you have an hour to kill, probably reading the paper or an old paperback book. The little bell over the door rings and I walk in, shaking my umbrella. What would you think?"

"I'd think that you shouldn't shake an umbrella inside because you're going to make the floor dangerously slippery for the next person who walks in."

She hits my arm playfully. "Come on, play along!" she says with a laugh. "What would you think about me?"

"Honestly?"

"Honestly."

I take a deep breath as I turn onto a dark road with no cars around. "I'd think that you were the most stunning woman I've ever seen. I'd think that I was dreaming. That I had died without knowing it and woke up in heaven."

"Would you be upset if I sat at your table and talked to you?"

"No. I'd be hoping you would."

She smiles as she watches me. She's turned in her seat now, her back against the door, those aroused-filled eyes locked on me. What the hell is she doing? Why is she making this so hard?

"What if we had a wonderful time?" she continues. "Would you ask for my number?"

"Every time with you would be wonderful."

"But would you ask for my number?"

"No."

Her mouth drops open with a playful scorned look on her face. She makes a scoff. "Why not?"

"Because you're my best friend's daughter and you're off-limits no matter what scenario we're in."

She crosses her arms over her chest as she narrows her eyes on me, looking like she's trying to figure me out.

"You're a lovely girl, Ruby," I say as I squeeze the wheel so hard my knuckles turn white, "but your father gave his life for mine and I'm not going to repay him by..."

"By what?" she asks, perking up in her seat and leaning over the middle console when I don't finish the thought. My heart starts pounding as she comes closer, putting those soft luscious lips an inch from my ear. Her breasts are pressing into my arm. She's *killing* me. "By doing what, Jack? Huh? What do you want to do to me?"

I clench my jaw as I try to focus on the road, but she smells so good and she's so damn soft. My cock is rock hard and *aching* with that sultry voice in my ear.

"I just want to get you home," I say in a deep scratchy voice.

"You want to get me home and do what?" she asks, her

voice dripping with lust. "What do you want to do to your baby girl?"

I'm breathing heavily as she slides her hand onto my hard stomach. Her breasts feel so good on my arm. Her soft hair is tickling my neck. I can't fucking think straight with those lips so close to me.

"Does it have to do with this?"

I drop my head and moan as that little hand slides down my clenched stomach and onto my hard cock. She rubs my thick shaft back and forth as she moans in my ear.

"Do you like that? Do you want me to put it in my mouth?"

"*Oh, fuck...*"

I'm trying to be good. I'm trying to stop her, but it's fucking impossible with her hand on me like this.

"Are you drunk?" I whisper.

"I'm drunk on loving you," she whispers. She starts kissing my cheek then my neck as she continues to stroke me. "I've been in love with you since I was a kid."

Oh, my god... What the fuck?

I can't do this, but it's all I want in the world.

I feel like I'm being turned and tousled and twisted up inside. I don't know what the fuck to do...

"*Oh fuck,*" I moan as she rubs my cock and kisses my neck. Her sweet succulent scent is filling my lungs with every breath I take, setting fire to my chest.

"But your father..." I whisper between quick breaths. "I can't do this to him."

"My father would want us both to be happy," she says between kisses. "Are you happy right now?"

"I've never been happier."

"And would you be happy if you had my wet warm lips wrapped around your big cock?"

My head drops back on the seat and I let out a low growl. I can't even with this girl. I'll take my chances in hell. It will be worth burning for an eternity for a few seconds of bliss with her.

Her father can find me in the afterlife if there is one and he can punish me for all of my sins. He can kill me all over again.

"*Yes,*" I gasp. "That would make me happy."

"Then, let me make you happy," she whispers as she kisses the corner of my mouth. "Let me make you *very* happy."

I watch in awe as she lowers herself onto my lap, pulling and clawing at my belt. She pulls the leather through the metal buckle, yanks the zipper down, and reaches her little hand into my pants.

A primal groan leaves my lips when I feel her soft skin on mine. She wraps her fingers around my throbbing shaft and pulls it out.

"*Oh,*" she says, shocked at the size. Her hand is gripping my thick base as she takes a long moment to admire it.

The back of my head is pressing against the seat as I drive down the long dark road, my hand gripping the steering wheel tight as she lowers her head and presses her soft plump lips against the swollen head of my cock. She gives it a soft kiss.

I know we shouldn't be doing this, but there's no stopping it now. We've crossed the line. There's no going back.

She opens her lips with a sexy moan and takes me into her mouth.

"Oh fuck," I groan when I feel her wet tongue on my head. She squeezes those lips tight around my throbbing shaft and slides them down, taking me in *deeper*.

"That's it, baby girl," I whisper as I feel her wet warm mouth engulfing me. "Just like that."

I slide one hand into her soft blonde hair and hold her head as she moves it up and down. It feels so *good*. So forbidden, which makes it that much dirtier. That much better.

I keep my half-closed eyes on the dark empty road as she starts sliding her clenched hand up my wet shaft, moving it at the same speed as her mouth.

She's mine now.

I don't care how wrong it is. I don't care what her father would think about it. Not anymore. Not after this.

I'm a greedy bastard who's going to take this angelic woman and keep her forever.

I'll protect her, shelter her, and take care of every single one of her needs.

She'll be mine and I'll be hers. For the rest of my days.

"Oh hell," I moan when she forces me in deep, taking as much of my big cock into her mouth as she can. "I'm going to fucking cum, baby girl."

Those words spur her on and she starts sucking and stroking me with a new intensity. I feel like I'm going to burst.

The tingle starts in my core and gets stronger as it plows through me, building in strength and intensity with each passing second.

I squeeze her head, hold her mouth down on my cock, and I cum *hard*.

"*Oh, fuck!*" I roar as I cum deep in this beauty's perfect little mouth.

That hot wet mouth never stops moving. She continues to suck and lick and swallow every drop I give her. It's so intense. It's so fucking good. I'm never letting this girl go. Never. She's all fucking mine.

The truck bumps and jerks as I accidentally roll onto the gravel shoulder of the road. Ruby gets up with a gasp.

"It's okay, baby girl," I whisper as I pull the truck back onto the paved road. "I just got a little distracted."

She leans back against the door, turned in her seat as she gazes at me with a lustful grin. She's smiling as she wipes her wet lips with her finger and then sucks on it.

My chest is moving up and down with every heavy breath. The intense orgasm she gave me is making my blood feel like thick syrup flowing through my veins.

"Are you happy now?" she asks with a sultry look.

"Yeah," I say as I slide my dick back into my pants and take a deep breath. "I don't think I've ever been this happy."

I turn and slowly look her up and down with dark hungry eyes. "When we get home, it's my turn to make you happy. *Very* happy."

She swallows hard as she watches me.

"It's going to be my first time," she says in a voice so low I'm not sure if I hear it correctly.

"You're a virgin?" I ask, turning to her in shock.

This girl is the most stunning woman on the planet. She could have anyone she wants. I still don't understand why she's choosing me...

"I've only wanted you, Jack," she whispers. "It's always been you. Even when I was a kid, I loved you. I wrote your name in my textbooks and stole a picture of you from my dad. I kept it hidden in my diary and would look at it every night. I'd dream about the day when I was older and we could finally be together."

"You don't have to dream anymore, baby girl. We're together now."

I reach over and grab her hand. She squeezes it and I hit the gas, racing up the mountain to get this girl alone.

To get her alone and to make her *mine*.

Chapter Nine

Jack

We're on each other before we even get into the house. She slams the door of the truck closed and runs into my arms. I catch her as she leaps on me, wraps her legs around my body, and crushes her lips to mine.

We don't hold back. I taste her mouth like I'm going to taste the dripping sweetness between her legs. She moans as I thrust my tongue in deep, tasting her, claiming her, making her mine.

Sorry, Derek. She belongs to me now.

I don't care if this is forbidden. The lure is too strong. The temptation unbearable. I'm taking this sweet girl and making her *mine.*

I grab her ass with my big strong hands and hold her spread pussy against me as she moans into my mouth. Her hands are sliding into my hair—grabbing and pulling desperately as she shoves her tongue into my mouth.

How can something so wrong feel so right?

It's like we were made for one another.

"*Inside*," she moans between kisses. "Bring me inside."

I carry her to the front door with my cock aching. She just drained my balls, but they're already full again and overflowing with the need to breed this young beauty.

She whimpers when I press her against the door and my hard dick digs into her pussy. Our mouths and tongues are still going at it—sloppy and wet, as I reach into my pocket and pull out my keys.

This girl is keeping me so distracted that it takes a few times fumbling with the key before I can get it into the lock. I finally turn it and open the door.

She kisses my face and neck as I carry her inside and kick the door closed behind me. A few of the lights are on, giving the place a nice warm glow.

Her legs unravel and she drops to her feet. I'm about to ask her what's wrong as she pulls away, but then I'm rendered speechless when she yanks her shirt over her head. Her blonde hair is a wild mess around her lust-filled eyes and wet tantalizing mouth.

My eyes drop to her chest and I groan in agony when I see her round perky breasts spilling out of her white lacy bra. She's so fucking hot. I want her naked. I want to see every delicious inch of her.

A primal growl rumbles out of my chest as I yank off my shirt and go to her. I grab her jaw, tilt her head back, and kiss her deep as she whimpers on my tongue.

I shuffle forward—and she shuffles back—until we bump into the stairs. I can't stop. Not now. My body is burning for her.

I pull back from her mouth and her teeth clamp onto my lower lip, tugging as I pull away. She releases me with a moan, those eager little hands on my belt again. She wants my big dick back inside her, but this time, between her legs. She'll get it, but I need to taste that sweet, soft, soaking virgin pussy first.

"Oh, Jack," she moans as I grab her breast and squeeze. I grab a fistful of her bra between her luscious tits and yank it down. Her bare breasts pop out and the most perfect pink nipples stare back at me. I lunge on them as I drop to a knee, sliding one into my mouth and sucking hard on the firm bud.

"*Yes*," she moans as she slides her fingers into my hair, holding me against her. "*Oh, fuck yes.*"

I switch to the other breast, rolling my tongue around her hard little nipple before I take it into my mouth and suck on it.

These are the most beautiful tits I've ever seen, but I need more right now. I need her virgin cunt on me.

I lick my way down her stomach as I pop open the button on her pants. She moans as I slide my hands into them and pull everything down—her pants, her panties —*everything*.

That hot wet cunt is right in front of my face as she steps out of her pants and gets naked. My mouth waters as I stare at her soft pink lips glistening with arousal.

As I stare at this forbidden tantalizing sight in front of me, I know I'm not going to make it up the stairs. I need her *now*.

"Sit, baby girl," I growl. "I'm going to taste you."

She's taking sharp quick breaths as she drops to the stairs, sitting with her legs closed. I kneel in front of her and place my palms on her knees.

Her lustful eyes are on me, but mine are locked on her juicy cunt as I slowly pry her legs open. She has blonde curls down there that look so incredibly soft. Her pussy lips are so pink. So wet. I open her legs wider and a bead of clear juice leaks out of her tight little opening.

Any control I was clinging to snaps. I lunge forward with a ravenous growl and drag my tongue up her wet honey-filled slit. She melts onto the stairs with a deep moan as my tongue slides over her clit.

She tastes like heaven. I can't get enough. I'm already addicted to her cunt. I know I'll be tasting her every day from now on.

I lick her again, and again, and again, sliding my tongue over every inch of her sweet pussy. I drag my tongue through her silky folds, around her clit, and plunge it into her tight virgin hole.

She grabs under her knees and holds her legs apart for me, not hiding a thing. My baby girl won't stop moaning. Her hips start rolling to the rhythm of my tongue.

"You like that, baby girl?" I ask, letting my heavy breath wash over her heat. She shivers from the sensation. "You like it when I lick your soft little pussy?"

"*Yes,*" she moans as her head drops back. Her hands are squeezed into fists. It's so intense for her.

I put my mouth back on her, rubbing her sweet pussy juice all over my lips and mustache. I want to smell her cunt as I'm driving my cock into it.

The more I lick her, the harder I get. My dick is *throbbing.* It's so hard it hurts.

"That's my girl," I whisper between strokes of my tongue. "Now, cum on me, baby. Cum all over your man's hungry mouth."

Her whimpers and moans increase in intensity as I

focus on her clit. I wrap my lips around it and suck hard. She screams out as I flick the hard pearl with my tongue and suck it in a rhythmic motion, desperate for her to cum all over me.

Those big beautiful tits bounce around as her body bucks and shakes. She grabs my hair and nearly pulls it out by the roots as her orgasm comes raging forward.

"*Yes,*" I growl. "Cum on me, baby girl."

My lips and tongue turn *ravenous*. I'm desperate to get her off.

"*Oh, Jack!*" she suddenly hollers as the orgasm hits and she's consumed by the heated bliss. Her body loses control as the waves of heat tear through her. Her legs tremble around me. She jerks and convulses as she cries out my name again.

Watching her cum is the sexiest thing I've ever seen. I'm torn between sitting back to watch or continuing to eat out this hot little pussy.

My girl takes the decision out of my hands and shoves her foot onto my shoulder. She pushes me away as she trembles violently, the sensations too much for her to handle.

I sit back and watch as she covers her face with her hands, breathing like she just ran up a mountain. Those gorgeous tits are heaving up and down, her pussy still glistening wet. I'm in love. I'm obsessed. How could I ever think I'd be able to resist her?

I'll never again be so stupid. I'll never turn this angel down again.

She drags her hands back over her hair as those stunning blue eyes lock onto me. "Let's go upstairs."

She turns around and when I see her irresistible ass in front of me, I lunge on it. I can't help it. She gasps in surprise, but that gasp quickly turns into moans as I tongue her cunt from behind, licking up her sweetness and then dragging my tongue up to her asshole. Her body shivers as I slide my wet tongue all over it.

I can't get enough of this girl. How the hell did I get through fifty-three years of life without her? I know I won't be able to get through fifty-three minutes without her again.

She presses her juicy cunt against my mouth for a bit and then suddenly bursts away from me, springing up the stairs and leaving me shocked at the bottom of the staircase.

I look up at her in desperation. My hard cock is making a mess in my pants, leaking out pre-cum everywhere.

"To be continued," she says with a grin as she takes off her bra and lets it drop onto the floor. "In the master bedroom."

My heart pounds as I watch her disappear into my room with a playful squeal. Her heady scent is still on my mouth, filling my lungs with every heavy breath I take.

With a primal growl, I run up the stairs and follow her into my room.

She's sitting on my bed—messy blonde hair on her shoulders, glazed-over eyes watching me, legs tucked together, breasts hanging free. I stop in the doorway to admire her for a second. Even though every cell in my being is screaming at me to claim her, I feast my eyes on the stunning sight for as long as I can.

I'll never see her like this again—so wholesome and pure. Untouched in her virginity. As soon as I step into this room, I'm going to take it from her.

It will be all fucking mine.

I try to memorize every ravishing detail—the grin on her red puffy lips, her perfect little toes on my bedspread, the curve of her spine, the long slender shape of her thighs, her straight white teeth, and those eyes... those fucking killer eyes...

The need to steal her virginity and breed her young ripe body becomes too much. I can't take it anymore.

I yank open my belt as I walk in, heading straight for her. My hard cock springs out as I pull down my pants and underwear. She watches as I wrap my hand around my thick shaft and start stroking as I step out of my pants, getting as naked as she is.

"Lay down." My grunts are barbaric. I don't even recognize my voice anymore. This forbidden beauty has brought me to a new place. A primal one that I haven't experienced before.

She drops onto her back and spreads her legs for me. I grab her hips and yank her forward until her ass is hanging off the bed.

I'm standing between her legs, watching with bated breath as I slide the thick head of my cock up her wet slit. Her warm pussy juice leaks onto my skin as I press my head to her tight virgin hole.

Our eyes meet.

This can't be wrong. It's too beautiful to be wrong.

She's my girl and I'm her man. I can see it now. There's no going back. No more shame. No more self-loathing. I'll do anything for this girl. I'll protect her from any threat. I'll be the man she needs.

I can't get her father's blessing, but I'll strive every day to be the man that she deserves. A man that my best friend would be proud to have as his daughter's partner.

Take her, a dark impatient voice roars inside me.

I grit my teeth and push my swollen head into her tight little pussy. She cries out and writhes on the bed as the head of my cock slides into her soft virgin heat.

"Oh shit," she cries out, her face twisting up as she feels my huge size stretching her out.

"It's okay, baby," I whisper as I cling to her legs and push in another inch. "It won't hurt for long."

I hope. This little pussy is so damn tight and my cock is not exactly small in length or thickness. The size difference between us has never been more apparent.

But she takes every inch without complaining. I stop pushing forward when I arrive at her cherry. My body shivers as I feel the firm resistance.

I knew she wasn't lying, but the confirmation that I'm the first man to be inside her fills me with pride and honor. She saved this sweet cherry for me and I'm going to *take* it.

I grit my teeth and thrust through it, giving her what she's been waiting for, what she's been *begging* for. My hard cock slides fully into her warm cunt and I hold it in there, listening to her whimper and moan as her pussy clamps down on my dick. She's so unbelievably tight. All I can focus on is the tight squeeze.

"That's it, baby girl," I whisper as I start rocking my hips, trying to loosen her up. Those big tits are jiggling with every movement. Her sexy moans are music to my ears. She's fucking perfect. "This little pussy is mine now. You're not leaving me, baby girl."

"I won't," she says in a breathless gasp. "I'm yours, Jack."

"That's right you are," I say with a dark possessive edge to my voice. "And this cock is right where it belongs. I just need to stretch your pussy out, baby. I need you to be brave."

"I can handle it, Jack," she says in a moan. "You don't have to go easy on me."

I grin as I spread her legs open and start pulling my hips

back, sliding my cock out of her tunnel. Just as the tip is about to slip out, I thrust back in, filling her back up.

She cries out, but she's rolling her hips and squeezing her breasts as she gets into it. Her cunt is so tight and this must be rough for her, but she's as strong as any man I've met.

A few more slow pumps of my hips and she's ready to go. Some of the intense tightness loosens and she takes me in easier.

We're not using any protection and I doubt an innocent virgin like her is on birth control.

I'll be aiming this load right at her young ripe womb. I want to *breed* this girl. I want her pregnant with my child. I want to fill this house with our babies until we have to move and get a bigger one.

Her back arches as I thrust in deep, sliding in and out of her heat with harder, longer strokes. Her pussy is clenched around my cock, *squeezing* and trying to pull the cum from my balls.

Her body wants to be bred as much as I want to breed it.

"Do you like feeling my dick in you?" I growl as I push every thick inch in, pressing the root of my cock against her pretty little pussy. "See how hard you make me, baby?"

"It feels so *good*," she moans as she grabs a fistful of the sheets.

I begin to move faster, sliding in with deeper, stronger strokes. I had planned to be soft and gentle for her first time, but I can't seem to stop myself from fucking her hard and fast. I keep spotting my hands on her—my fingertips digging too hard into her flesh.

I need to calm down a little. I don't want to hurt her.

I pull back, holding just an inch or two inside.

Those alert blue eyes dart onto me. "What is it?"

"I'm trying to control myself," I say, taking sharp breaths. "I don't want to hurt you."

"Don't stop, Jack," she begs. "You could never hurt me."

She wraps her legs around my ass and pulls me back into her. I grin as I watch her begging for it. She's got her father's toughness, that's for sure.

I let her have it, fucking her hard until this pretty little pussy is cumming all over me. She screams and convulses, her sexy little body bucking on the bed as the heat floods her insides.

This tight cunt clenches around me, squeezing my shaft as she cums. It feels incredible.

"That's my good girl," I whisper as she settles down, the orgasm fading through her. "Now turn around for your man."

I pull my hard dick out of her and look down at her pink virgin cream coating my shaft. She hops onto her hands and knees, oblivious to the beautiful sight I'm gazing at. I grab her ass with a firm grip as I climb onto the bed, ready to take her from behind.

She drops her head and moans like she's in heaven as I slide my cock back into her.

Breeding her is the only thing on my mind now.

I grab her ass cheeks way too hard and slam my cock into her over and over until the bed is skirting across the room and her cries of pleasure are bouncing off the walls.

She's *mine*.

I'm going to claim her womb just like I'm claiming her cunt.

The thought of her pregnant... walking around my house with a big belly and hard full tits... I growl as I thrust in with no holding back.

It doesn't take long before we're both ready to erupt.

"Oh, Jack!" she screams. "I'm going to cum!"

My eyes are locked on her juicy cunt. Hot juice is leaking everywhere as I fuck her. It's dripping down my full balls and spraying onto my muscular thighs. She's so *wet*. So *ready*.

I grit my teeth as an orgasm comes charging out of the darkness. I hold it back with a growl.

"Cum on me, baby girl. "Cum all over my cock."

She throws her head back and lets out a roar as her pussy cums all over my shaft. The sudden tightness sets me off and I lodge my dick deep into her and release.

The intensity staggers me. I cling to her as it sears through my body, better than any feeling I've had before.

Hot streams of cum shoot out of my cock and into her, heading straight to her willing womb.

I hope that will do it. I hope that will get her bred.

My cock jerks one last time and the last bit of my seed enters her body.

I pull out of her and she collapses on the bed, moaning and breathing heavily and making no effort to cover herself.

I sit back and look her over from her wild blonde hair, down her curved spine, over her gorgeous ass that still has my red fingerprints on it, and then onto her soft puffy pussy that's leaking out my cum.

She's mine now.

I finally have the girl of my dreams.

At fifty-three years old, it took long enough.

But my Ruby was worth the wait.

I'm just glad the wait is over.

Chapter Ten

Ruby

"And what about this one?" I ask with a smile as I touch a two-inch scar on Jack's stomach with my fingertip.

We're laying in bed in the morning—him on his back, me on my stomach—and I'm going through his history, one scar at a time.

"That was an extraction mission," he says as he runs his hand through his beard. "I can't tell you the country, but it was a jungle and it was hot."

I'm resting on my elbows with his bedsheet halfway up my back. I can't get enough of this. I don't think I'll ever get tired of listening to Jack talk and tell old stories like this.

"Was my father there?"

"Yeah," he says as he looks at me with a smile. "He was there, leading the pack as usual."

I love that we can talk about my father now and not get

upset. I want to hear all these old stories about him and I don't want any tears to ruin them.

"We were tasked to retrieve an Air Force pilot who was taking pictures of a drug lab deep in the jungle when he had a mechanical failure and went down. The drug smugglers got him and were holding him prisoner. We had to sneak in and get him out."

My heart picks up as I imagine Jack in his youth, wearing that sexy uniform and charging into one dangerous situation after another. He's the bravest man I know.

"We got to the holding cell in the middle of the night and snuck in to grab him. Your dad took out both of the guards. I probably shouldn't be telling you this..."

"No, it's okay. Don't leave anything out. I want to hear it."

He looks at me for a moment and then sighs. "They were bad men, Ruby. They were harassing the villagers nearby and had half of the men from the village locked up with the pilot. It was bad."

"What did you do?"

"Our mission was to retrieve the pilot only. Get in and out undetected, but that all changed when some fucker came charging out of the darkness, high as shit and hollering like a banshee. He stabbed me right here while I was picking a lock."

I run my tingling fingertips over the faded line on his soft warm skin, so happy and thankful that he survived.

"This mean fucker on our team named Grouch took him out easily, but I was in bad shape. On my ass and bleeding like a broken pipe while every drug smuggler in the area came barrelling down on us."

"That must have been terrifying."

He runs his hand through his hair and shrugs like it was nothing.

"It wasn't?"

He exhales hard as he looks at me. "You have to understand... Back then... It wasn't scary to us. It was just another day at the office. That's what we did. It was... fun."

"Fun?!"

He laughs as he looks at me. "Yeah. Fun."

Speaking of fun... I want to have some.

I crawl to him, letting the cool bed sheet slide over my ass.

The look in his eyes turns from amusement to hunger as I get up and straddle his body. His strong hands cup my tingling breasts as I pull the sheet off his lap. I moan when he squeezes them, showing me his incredible strength.

"I'm glad you made it out," I say as I slide my wet pussy onto his firm shaft. He moans as I grind against it. "I'm glad you're still in one piece."

"Which piece are you most glad for?" he asks in a deep throaty voice.

I reach down and grab his thick long dick which is soaked with my hot juices. "This one."

We both moan as I arch my hips up, guide his beautiful cock to my opening, and slide it inside. I'm in heaven as I sink down on it, feeling the firm length penetrating *deep* inside me.

He's *so* big. He's a mountain of a man.

And he's all mine.

I grab onto his broad shoulders and start riding him, moving my hips up and down at a fast pace.

His ravenous brown eyes are fixated on my breasts as they bounce up and down in front of his face. I love fucking this man. I want him inside me every day from now on.

Those big hands slide onto my ass and he starts moving me up and down like he's jerking himself off with my pussy.

I'm so wet. It's gushing out of me and making a mess all over his pelvis, his cock, and his big masculine balls.

"God, your pussy is good," he growls as I push down on him and grind my clit on his hard pelvis. "You're incredible, baby girl."

I love it when he calls me that. I've always wanted to be his baby girl.

I ride him again until we're both crying out and cumming all over each other. I scream out his name as the orgasm burns through me like sweet bliss.

His hot cum coats the inside of my pussy as I collapse onto his chest and he wraps those big arms around me. I'm trembling as he holds me tight.

It should be perfect, but there's an uneasy feeling gnawing at the back of my mind.

Something unsettling has been hovering in my head all morning. It only hits when Jack gets up to make us coffee and I'm lying in bed by myself.

"The picture! Shit!"

I leap out of bed, wrap Jack's humongous robe around me, and race down to the kitchen.

He smiles when he sees me and the beautiful sight of him shirtless in his black boxer briefs making coffee in his kitchen is so heart-stopping that it makes me forget all about my worries. But just for a second.

"Can I use your computer?" I ask him, trying to hide the panic in my voice.

"It's in my office," he says. "Help yourself."

I race up the stairs and into his office. I go straight to the laptop on his desk and pull up my Facebook page.

"Shit! No, no, no, no, no!"

A picture of me and Michele at the bar last night is on my page. She tagged me in it.

Look who I ran into at the Cliffside Tavern in the Greene Mountains!

She even put my location. I'm so screwed! I immediately untag myself and send her a message to please delete it, but she had posted it last night shortly after we ran into each other.

Crenshaw's girlfriend's warnings ring in my ears as I drop down on the desk chair, feeling like I might be sick.

No real names, no social media, no phones. He'll track you down with it... He's relentless. He's merciless.

And now I've gone and put Jack in danger too. This is not good.

"Everything okay?" he asks at the door. "I heard you swearing."

I can't even look at him. I'm too ashamed. How could I be so freaking stupid? I shouldn't have taken a picture with Michele. She puts *everything* on social media!

"I messed up."

He walks over and sits on the desk in front of me.

"What happened?"

I show him the picture of me with the town name right under it. "The guys who are after me are going to come here now. They're going to find me."

"No," he says as he turns the laptop toward him and starts clicking around. "They're going to find me."

"That's even worse!"

"Post this picture," he says as he turns the laptop back around. It's a picture of me from yesterday with Jack's house in the background. "And write something like, 'Having fun on Silvergray Mountain!'"

My face drops as I stare at him in horror. "Are you crazy? They'll come right to your doorstep!"

"Exactly."

I shake my head as I stare at him in disbelief. "No! Why?"

"They're coming to the town anyway, right?"

"Yeah."

"I can't have them around you, baby girl. I can't put you in an unsafe position like that. I'll put you up in the beautiful lodge in town and meanwhile, we'll draw them here."

My face must look horrified as I stare at him because he chuckles.

"I'm sorry," he says, taking my hand. "I didn't mean to laugh."

"How can you be so calm about this?!" I screech. "These men will come to your house!"

"I want them to come," he says calmly.

He *wants* them to come? He is crazy.

"This is what I do, baby girl," he says in a soft, calm voice. "This is what I was made for. What I trained all those years for—to keep you safe."

I shake my head in disbelief as I stare at the computer screen. "I can't do it."

"Then, let me." He takes the laptop and posts the picture, tagging his mountain in the description.

I drop my head, feeling like I'm going to faint. This is the opposite of what I wanted.

He gently touches my chin and raises my head until I'm looking into his eyes. "I can't have any threats around you, Ruby. It's my job to eliminate them all. You're my girl now, and I'm going to keep you safe."

I want to believe him, but this is just terrifying. After a

lifetime of yearning, I finally have Jack and I don't want to lose him.

"It's going to be okay," he whispers as he leans down and softly kisses my lips. "Don't worry about a thing. I'll keep you safe."

I'm not even worried about me anymore.

I just want him to be okay.

———

"Are you sure about this?" I ask Jack as we walk into the gorgeous Greene Mountain Lodge. This place is stunning with a huge majestic fireplace in the middle of the lobby and luxurious everything. I've never been in a place this nice before, but I'm too nervous to enjoy it. All I can think about is Crenshaw and his goons arriving at Jack's house.

"Please trust me on this," he says, cupping my cheeks and looking into my eyes. "Everything will be okay. I've faced off against much worse men than this Crenshaw punk. I'm a Navy SEAL remember."

I swallow hard as he kisses my forehead and then walks to the counter. A pair of identical twins are behind it, both with black bobs and black-rimmed glasses.

"Hello," Jack says to them.

They both take their time to look up, but their mouths drop in shock when they see Jack. They're both staring at him with wide unblinking eyes.

"I'd like to book a room. The nicest one you have."

Neither of them says a word. They just stare up at him in awe.

Jack waits for them to answer, but there's just more staring. I think these girls have a thing for older men.

I roll my eyes as I look at their name tags—Tina and Tiffany.

"Do you want company?" Tina eagerly says. "I get off in an hour."

"What?" Jack says, jerking his head back in shock. "No."

"How about me?" Tiffany says as she takes off her glasses and fluffs her hair. "I'll rock your world, old man. You'll have to use a walker after I'm done with you."

"Wha—?" Jack looks so confused.

"He already has company," I say as I wrap my arms around his and hold it while glaring at them. "Just a room would be fine, please and thank you."

They both narrow their eyes at me. I narrow mine back at them. It's a stare-off until the manager named Lauren sees and comes rushing over.

"Girls, why don't you take a break?" Lauren says as she hurries around the desk.

"We're good," Tina says, still glaring at me.

"Yeah, we're *really* good," Tiffany says as she gives Jack a salacious look.

"*Girls*," Lauren snaps. "Take a break. *Now*."

They slowly get up while shamelessly drinking Jack in with hungry eyes. I stare them down until they disappear into the back.

"Sorry about them," Lauren says, laughing nervously. "They get a little weird around older men. Now, what can I do for you?"

She gives us a nice room and even gives us a discount so we'll hopefully forget all about the creeps at the front desk.

The enormity of the situation hits me once again when we're riding the elevator up to our floor.

I look up at Jack, wanting to cry.

"It's okay," he whispers as he tucks a strand of hair behind my ear. "They'll never bother you again after tonight."

I want to believe him, it's just... my luck is so horrible.

My stomach is in knots as we walk to the room. I open the door and gasp when I see the stunning view from the window.

Jack has his hungry eyes on me.

As soon as the door closes, those big hands are on me, picking me up and carrying me to the bed. He tosses me onto the mattress and yanks off his shirt.

"Oh boy," I whisper as he comes over with a sexy look. "Did those twins get you in the mood or something?"

He laughs and the deep booming sound makes me feel a little better. "You're the only one who gets me in the mood, baby girl."

I open my legs and he comes crawling between them with a killer look. I hope he remembered to put the *Do Not Disturb* sign on the door, because I don't want to be interrupted...

Chapter Eleven

Jack

As night falls, I get ready.

It's like old times as I suit up in my old black camo gear and strap my bulletproof vest over my shoulders. It all still fits.

I wish Derek was here with me. We'd always crack each other up as we got ready for a mission. He was the funniest motherfucker alive.

"I'll take care of your little girl," I whisper to him, wherever he is.

I'm not going to feel bad anymore. Ruby and I belong together. We were made for one another.

Fate brought her to my doorstep and I'm done pretending like I'm going to turn her away. I'll be the protector she needs. I'll kill any man who comes to harm what's mine.

My heart pumps with excitement as I open the old jar and feel the thick black paste on my fingertips.

I've been longing for this. I'm a born warrior and warriors need a purpose. We need to feel useful. We need someone to protect.

I slide my fingers into the thick paste and spread it over my face, feeling the nostalgic excitement of anticipation before a battle returning into my bones.

When I'm done, I wash my hands in the sink and look at my dark reflection in the mirror.

"Let's do this for Ruby. Let's do this for Derek. Let's do this for you."

I dig my fist into my palm and grin.

I'm ready.

Let them come.

———

The black Hummer pulls into my driveway and five guys spill out. It's around two in the morning with overcast skies. There's barely a shred of light up here beyond their headlights and these idiots didn't think to bring flashlights. This is going to be easy.

I'm halfway up a tree, sitting on a thick branch while I wait for them to disperse.

Half of them turn on the flashlights on their phones. Are they trying to stand out?

I guess they're not used to being the hunted. They're used to be the feared tough guys, getting little to no resistance.

Well, up here in the mountains, it's different. Up here, *I'm* the hunter.

They have no idea that they just stepped into an arena with a monster.

My eyes narrow on Crenshaw. Ruby gave me a description of him—slicked back greasy hair, pale skin, cheap black suit. I spot him immediately as he gets out of the passenger seat of the Hummer. Rage surges through my veins as he starts barking out orders and then charges up to the house. Three of them walk around the house, two on the left and one on the right. The fat one lingers by the car.

I'll take him out first.

He lights a smoke as Crenshaw opens the unlocked front door of my house and slips inside.

This lazy fuck is so unconcerned about someone fighting back that he leans on the bumper and starts scrolling through his phone.

I climb down the tree and drop to my feet without making a sound. I have a handgun in my belt, but I pull out my knife instead. No need to alert the others just yet.

It's so dark out and this guy is blinded by the bright screen that I can walk right up to him in my black gear without being spotted.

I slap the phone out of his hands and he looks up at me with a gasp. I don't hesitate. My hand strikes like a cobra and the long sharp knife sinks into his jugular.

He stares at me with wide terrified eyes as I yank the blade back out.

Hot blood sprays everywhere. He clutches his bloody neck, but it's over so fast. He falls to his knees as the life leaves his eyes and then his lifeless body slams face first into the dirt.

His back leg twitches for a few seconds, but after that, he stops moving.

I'm already on my way around the house. I head left

where the pair of thugs went. One is standing on his toes and looking into the window. I squeeze the handle of my knife and head right for him.

"Looking for something?" I whisper in a growl as I grab his shoulder. He looks back in shock. I shove the blade into his kidney and cover his mouth with my gloved hand as his muffled screams turn to gurgles.

"What the fuck?!" his buddy shouts when he comes around the corner of the house and sees me killing his friend.

He suddenly remembers he's got a gun in his hand and raises it. I yank the knife out and launch it at him as hard as I can. He jerks to the side at the last second and the blade grazes his shoulder.

Shit, I must be getting slower in my old age. The younger version of me would never have missed an easy shot like that. Derek would be laughing his ass off if he could see me now.

The guy recovers and points the gun at me. I hold his friend up, ducking behind him as six shots ring out. They all land in my human shield's chest. He goes limp in my hands as I pull out my own gun.

This time, I don't miss. I get the shooter clean in the head with one shot, killing him instantly.

I guess I'm not that slow after all.

"What's happening?!" the guy on the other side of the house hollers. "Ivan! Michael! Where are you?"

I let go of the dead body in my hand and he falls to the ground.

"Talk to me!" the guy hollers in a frantic voice as I sneak around the front of the house toward him. I'm staying in the shadows, which makes me practically invisible with my dark outfit and black makeup. Him, not so much. He's waving the light on his cell phone around as he swings his gun frantically from side to side.

"What the *fuck* is happening out here?!" Crenshaw bellows from a window on the top floor. It's Ruby's room.

I grit my teeth as rage rips through my veins, knowing that fucker is in my baby girl's room. It's time to end this shit now.

I shoot the frantic guy twice. Once in the chest and once in the head as he falls down.

"Christoff!" Crenshaw shouts as the gunshots echo through the mountains. "Christoff, you good?"

"They're all dead!" I shout back in a deep primal voice. "Come down here, you're next."

"Oh, fuck," I hear him mutter. "Who the hell are you?"

"The angel of death," I holler back. "The eater of souls. I'm the man who's going to take your life for trying to hurt my girl."

"Come and get it," he shouts before firing blindly into the night sky.

That's it, asshole. Waste all those bullets...

The firing stops.

I crouch down in the shadows, waiting for him to make the next move.

Besides the buzzing and crackling of insects, it's silent up here.

My body is screaming at me to go and take him out, but I sit and wait, listening for a door to open.

I would have already been recklessly hunting him down in my youth, but in my youth, I didn't have Ruby. I didn't have someone amazing like her waiting for me to return home safely. I didn't have a bright future like I do now.

I have to be smart. And careful. I have to return to my girl in one piece.

The back door slams shut and I burst into action, hurrying around the house with my gun drawn.

I peek around the house to the backyard with my pulse racing. It's empty. *Where the fuck is he?*

I'm scanning the dark trees when I hear a gun cock behind me.

My blood goes cold.

"Drop it."

Shit.

How the hell did this punk sneak up on me? I must be getting old.

Derek wouldn't be laughing now. I'm in it bad.

I raise my hands and slowly turn around.

"I said drop the fucking gun!" Crenshaw roars. "Are you deaf, old man?!"

Our eyes meet. My heart pounds violently as I stare him down.

"Drop it!"

I let go of the gun and it falls to the ground with a clatter.

"Back up!"

I take a few steps back and he grabs my gun and stuffs it into his belt.

This fucker is trying to kill my Ruby. He doesn't know how dead he is.

"What's that shit on your face?" he says, pointing the gun at me. "Fucking crazy mountain weirdos. Where's the girl? Where's Ruby?"

"Ruby is *my* girl."

"Tell me where she is or I'll put one through your heart!"

"You're going to need more than that gun to stop me."

"Fine," he says with his eyes narrowing. "Have it your way."

He fires until the gun runs out of bullets. The flashes light up my backyard as four bullets slam into my chest, knocking the breath out of my lungs.

The impact throws me backward and I hit the house. I fall to my knee, gasping for breath as he turns and hurries into the front.

He thinks he's killed me.

He doesn't know I'm wearing a bulletproof vest.

Those bullets stung like hell and I'll be bruised up pretty bad tomorrow, but they didn't pierce my skin.

I get up and go after him.

"Shit!" I hear him shout on the other side of the house. "Useless fucking idiots!"

He must have found the two guys I took out.

I take off after him. This time, I'm not silent. I don't take it slow. I channel some of the crazy alpha energy I had in my youth and sprint around the house and charge right for the fucker.

He gasps in shock when he sees me and tries to go for my gun tucked in his belt. I crack him right in the face with a hard punch before he can get it out. He stumbles back with a grunt.

I don't let up. I slam my fist into his stomach and then into his face.

He stumbles back as blood bursts from his nose.

"Is anyone else after her?" I ask as I stalk him down. He stumbles into one tree and then another as he tries to get away from me.

"Fuck you!"

"Wrong answer."

I slam my fist into his cheek and he stumbles back.

"Is anyone else after my Ruby?" I ask again.

"Just me," he growls as he spits a wad of blood out of his mouth while glaring at me. "And when I find her... I'm really going to have some fun. You messed with the wrong fucking guy, old man."

He grabs the gun tucked into his pants with a sinister grin on his face.

A sliver of moon is shining through the clouds. It glints on a blade stuck in the tree beside me. It's the ax that Ruby aimed at the target, but missed wildly.

"I'll give Ruby your regards," he says as he points the gun at my face. "When I'm fucking her and slitting her throat."

That's enough.

This ends now.

I leap to the side, snatch the ax out of the tree, and launch it at him in one lightning-fast motion. The ax summersaults through the air and sinks into the middle of his chest.

He doesn't get a shot off.

Crenshaw drops to his knees as I walk over, staring him down.

I yank the ax out of his chest with a grunt and hold it to his throat.

"You fucked with the wrong girl," I growl. "She's mine."

He looks at me with pleading eyes, but there's no mercy when it comes to ending threats to my girl.

I slice him open, so my girl can be free.

Chapter Twelve

Ruby

This has been the longest night of my life. It's nine in the morning and I'm still pacing around, worried sick about Jack.

I don't know how my mother did it for all those years. She must have been going crazy at home while my father was out on mission after mission, not knowing if he'd ever come back.

I have a newfound respect for her. This is tough. I haven't slept at all.

"You have to pace yourself," I remind myself in front of the mirror. "It might take Crenshaw a few days before he arrives and you might have a lot more nights like this."

I take a few deep breaths, but they do nothing to calm my wrecked nerves.

This is all my fault. I came here and put Jack in danger. No matter what he says, his life *is* in danger and it's because

.ie. If something happens to him, I'll never forgive
.myself.

I lie on the bed and stare at the ceiling, wondering
what's going to happen next. What am I going to do if Jack
does take care of Crenshaw and his crew? Am I just
supposed to pack up and return home like none of this ever
happened?

A knock on the door jerks me up and sends my heart
rocketing. I rush over to the door, look through the peep-
hole, and nearly burst into tears when I see Jack standing in
the hallway.

I yank the door open and leap into his arms, wrapping
my legs around his waist as I breathe in his masculine scent
with tears in my eyes.

"You're okay," I whisper into his neck.

His arms tighten around me and he carries me back into
the room, kicking the door closed behind him.

"Of course, I'm okay. I told you I'd protect you."

I drop to my feet and look him over. He has some
smudges of black makeup on his face near his hairline and
by his ears. His clothes are clean, but he has lines of black
soil under his fingernails and he looks exhausted. Something happened.

"Did... Crenshaw come?" I ask, not wanting to say his
name.

Jack nods.

I swallow hard, waiting for him to elaborate, but he
doesn't. "*And?!*"

"He's not going to bother you anymore, baby girl. Him
or his friends."

"But how can you be so sure?" I ask. "He's relentless.
He's merciless. He's—"

"Buried in the mountains where no one will ever find him."

My body suddenly goes weak as all of the tension I've been holding releases like the wind. I stumble back and sit on the bed as that beautiful relief sinks in.

Crenshaw is dead. I don't have to worry about him ever again.

I slowly look up at Jack, not knowing what to say or how to express the tremendous sense of gratitude I'm feeling right now. I'm free because of him.

A nagging worry begins to worm its way into my mind. "The police?"

"Will never find him," Jack says with a confident nod. "My friend Stan owns a construction company with lots of heavy machinery. He helped me out."

"Oh," I say when it clicks. They must have buried them deep in the ground somewhere out in the wilderness. If Jack says it's okay, then I'll have to believe him. He is a professional in this area after all.

"Thank you, Jack," I whisper as I look up at him. "You're my hero."

He gives me a tired smile that makes me all tingly inside.

"I guess there's nothing stopping me... from... going home."

That smile quickly disappears. "I'm stopping you."

A warmth fills my chest. That's just what I wanted to hear.

"Are you going to keep me here as your prisoner?"

"I'm going to keep you here as my girl."

A slow smile builds on my face as I watch him.

"It doesn't matter that I'm older, Ruby. It doesn't matter that your father was my best friend. We belong together, ѕrl. You and me forever. Don't go back. Stay with me. ʟy with me and we'll start a new life. We're better together, you know that."

It's not even a choice. I'll pick him over anything.

"Okay, Jack," I say with flushed cheeks and a big smile. "I'll stay and be your baby girl."

He lunges forward, cups my cheeks, and kisses me like I've never been kissed before.

I moan as I fall back on the bed, pulling him on top of me.

We better add a few more nights to our booking...

We're going to need it.

Epilogue

Jack

Nine months later...

Ruby bends over in the passenger seat and wails like a wounded buffalo. She's clutching her swollen belly as I speed up even faster.

"You're doing amazing, baby girl," I tell her as I hold her hand. She's squeezing it so hard that it hurts. I didn't know my girl was this strong.

The contraction passes and she sinks into the seat, breathing heavily with sweat beading on her forehead.

"Are you okay?"

"Yeah," she says in a breathless tone. "Just don't stop."

I hate to see her in pain like this. If I could take it from her and experience it myself instead, I would.

I would do anything for her.

s given me so much. She's given me a new start. A
lease on life.

Before she arrived on my doorstep, I was drinking too
much, smoking too much, and fighting too much—all things
that were bad for me.

But ever since she stepped back into my life, I haven't
touched any of it. Not one drop of alcohol, not one inhale of
a cigarette, and not one trip back to The Cracked Barrel
Saloon for Fight Night. Stan has been begging me to return
—he always bet heavily on my fights and always made out
well—but that dark part of my life is done.

All of the darkness is over.

I'm a man who's seen a lot of darkness throughout his
years, but Ruby is my light. She's the light that guides
me now.

"*Oww!!*" she screams as another contraction hits. Her
face twists up and she grits her teeth as she powers
through it.

It kills me to see her like this. I hate to see her in pain.

I love her so damn much. I'm utterly obsessed with this
girl.

The past nine months have been pure bliss. Just having
her in my house where I can look out for her was good
enough, but then she told me she was pregnant and my
whole world was rocked.

I loved seeing her stomach get larger over the past few
months, knowing my baby was growing in her womb. We
couldn't keep our hands off each other this whole time.

She wanted to get a job in town, but I didn't want her
working while she was pregnant, so I surprised her one
day by converting a spare room into an office for her
custom sticker company. I blindfolded her and brought
her in. She was so thrilled when I showed her. I had done

a lot of research to find out the best sticker-making equipment and I bought it all for her. The top-of-the-line printer, cutter, and all of the various inks and sticker paper she could dream of. I even bought her a new laptop.

She instantly restarted her business and it's been going great. She gets orders every day.

"The hospital is just up ahead," I say as I race toward it. "We're almost there."

The excitement is building within as I park the truck and race to get a wheelchair. I can't wait to see my baby. We're having a girl.

Ruby likes Aurora for a name, but I like Jessica.

Either way, I just hope she's healthy. Nothing matters more than that. She'll be loved by both her parents no matter what her name is.

I get Ruby into the wheelchair and roll her up to the maternity ward.

The labor is really short after that. We barely get her into the room before the baby comes shooting out.

She's so beautiful. I'm already in love.

I'm holding her tiny body and staring at her perfect face in awe.

I can't wait for it all. The cuddles, piggyback rides, dance recitals, and food fights. I even can't wait for the dirty diapers, temper tantrums, and messy house. I'm just so excited for this blessed new life I didn't think I'd ever be lucky enough to have.

"How about Amelia?" Ruby asks in a whisper.

I smile as I look at my baby sleeping in my big hands.

"She looks like an Amelia," I whisper. "I like it."

"Come here," Ruby says, waving me onto the hospital bed.

down beside her and we both watch the baby sleep-
knowing that nothing will ever be the same again.

We have a family now. *I* have a family.

I'm so grateful for these two new angels in my life.

A life that I thought was over.

It's not over anymore.

It's only just beginning...

Epilogue

Ruby

Ten Years Later...

"**L**ook at what your daughter is doing," I say with a laugh when I spot Amelia out the window over the kitchen sink.

"Where did she find that?" Jack asks with a chuckle as he comes to my side and watches her. "I put that away years ago."

Our adorable little ten-year-old is standing a few yards in front of the wooden target with the bullseye on it. She has a fierce determined look on her face as she lines up the throwing ax and then launches it as hard as she can. It slams into the middle of the bullseye with a *thunk*.

We both laugh out of shock.

"She takes after you," I say as I look up at my man.

...make an amazing Navy SEAL one day," Jack ...s he watches her with a warm smile.

I shake my head, not even wanting to think about that. Two Navy Seals in my family are enough for me.

"Seal!" our one-and-a-half-year-old Max shouts from his high chair. "Seal! Seal! Seal!"

Jack turns to him with a raised eyebrow. "Maybe we'll have two Navy SEALs..."

"He's talking about *real* seals," I say with a laugh as Jack goes and picks him up. "The animal, but nice try."

I lean against the counter and smile as I watch Jack lift Max up and blow a raspberry on his stomach. He squeals in delight.

We have three children—Amelia, our middle son James who's playing upstairs in his room, and little Max.

Jack is the most caring, loving, and attentive father out there. He's such a wonderful man and I'm so happy that he's mine.

I always feel so safe and secure with him looking out for our family. We all have our own personal Navy SEAL bodyguard looking out for us.

Another ax hits the wooden target with a *thunk*.

"Is she okay playing with those?" I ask nervously as I peek out the window. She got it in the bullseye again! What the hell? I missed it by a mile my first time trying that. She really is her father's daughter.

"Oh yeah," Jack says like it's nothing. "I taught her how to properly handle a blade years ago."

I close my eyes and shake my head, not wanting to hear any of *that*.

When you have a Navy SEAL *slash* Mountain Man husband, you quickly learn that you have to let some things slide.

At least I know that my children will know how to protect themselves when that inevitable day comes when they venture out on their own.

I'll be sad to see them go, but at least I'll still have Jack.

My savior. My mountain man. My soul mate.

And he will *always* be enough.

The End!

More Mountain Men!

Lost In The Mountains

Desire In The Mountains

Passion In The Mountains

Found In The Mountains

Grumpy In The Mountains

Yearning In The Mountains

Mountain Man Fixated

Mountain Man Rescued

Mountain Man Taken

My Mountain Man Muse

Mountain Man Box Set

All in Kindle Unlimited!

Come and join my private Facebook Group!

Become an OTT Lover!

www.facebook.com/groups/OTTLovers

Become Obsessed with OTT

Sign up to my mailing list for all the latest OTT news and get a free book that you can't find anywhere else!

This man breathes power.

OBSESSED
By Olivia T. Turner
A Mailing List Exclusive!

When I look out my office window and see her in the next building, I know I have to have her.

ﺑle damn company she works for just to be

ﺑ going to be in my office working under me.
ﺑnder, over, sideways—we're going to be working together in *every* position.
This young innocent girl is going to find out that I work my employees *hard*.
And that her new rich CEO is already beyond *obsessed* with her.

This dominant and powerful CEO will have you begging for overtime! Is it just me or is there nothing better than a hot muscular alpha in a suit and tie!
All my books are SAFE with zero cheating and a guaranteed sweet HEA. Enjoy!

Go to www.OliviaTTurner.com to get your free ebook of Obsessed

Audiobooks

Check out my complete collection of audiobooks at
www.OliviaTTurner.com!

I'm adding more of your favorite OTT stories all the time!

Come Follow Me...

www.OliviaTTurner.com

facebook.com/OliviaTTurnerAuthor

instagram.com/authoroliviatturner

goodreads.com/OliviaTTurner

amazon.com/author/oliviatturner

bookbub.com/authors/olivia-t-turner

Made in the USA
Middletown, DE
06 September 2023